IF ALL ELSE FAILS . . .

IF ALL ELSE FAILS...

CRAIG STRETE

With an introduction by
Jorge Luis Borges

DOUBLEDAY & COMPANY, INC.
GARDEN CITY, NEW YORK
1980

"To See the City Sitting on Its Buildings," copyright © 1975 by U.P.D.
Publishing Corp.
"A Horse of a Different Technicolor," copyright © 1975 by U.P.D. Pub-
lishing Corp.
"Time Deer," copyright © 1974 by U.P.D. Publishing Corp.
"With the Pain It Loves and Hates," copyright © 1976 by Scholastic
Magazines, Inc.
"Who Was the First Oscar to Win a Negro?" copyright © 1975 by Damon
Knight.
"Why Has the Virgin Mary Never Entered the Wigwam of Standing Bear?"
copyright © 1975 by Fawcett Publications, Inc.
"Your Cruel Face," copyright © 1976 by Computer Decisions, Hayden
Publishing Co.
"When They Find You," copyright © 1977 by Greenwillow Books.
"The Bleeding Man," copyright © 1974 by U.P.D. Publishing Corp.; 1977
by Greenwillow Books.

First Edition

ISBN: 0-385-15237-x
Library of Congress Catalog Card Number: 79-7117
Copyright © 1980 by Craig Strete
All Rights Reserved
Printed in the United States of America

CONTENTS

INTRODUCTION:
NOTES ON A
DANGEROUS WRITER

I would like to introduce you to a collection of small nightmares of great consequence. My most startling discovery in
a recent trip to the United States was the writer whose
works are now before you. His discovery (one of the focal
points of my obsessions is that perhaps it was I who was discovered) encompassed a certain pervasive amount of envy
in me.

In my histories of nightmares I myself am about to dream,
T would like to have written (and perhaps I will) some of
the nightmares in this book.

Witnessing the birth of a new voice in literature requires
a different sort of compassionate appreciation. We must approach the birth of a new kind of dream, never dreamt until
this moment, without caution or reproach.

What is before us? What new thing in a world without
new things? Detailed myths, relived tribal epiphanies, du-
plicated realities that were once closed off, walled off into a
conspiracy of isolation.

These are prenightmares from the approaching Ice Age of
the lost, the damned, the cruelly assimilated, Los Indios.
These stories before you, like shattered chains of brilliance,
are therefore all the more awesome. The reality of Los
Indios, the American Indian you would call him in your
country, is both terrifying and beautiful. Perhaps it is even
fatal.

These stories, then, are like harps of temptations, thrumming with the crude power of an undiscovered cosmos. To be heard by us, cowering like tamed beasts behind the walls of our curiously mundane civilizations, the player of this orchestra of harps must have a special, prophetic genius, else we would never hear the notes he chooses to play.

And how brilliantly the melody anticipates us in these stories! We are in the presence of a beautiful performer, within whose voice we find absent our own standards and pantomimed mythologies. What is the world herein depicted, its absences and excesses?

Of its excesses, I know nothing or very little. This is a newer reality and we can only catalogue it by what is missing. For example, in this writer's wanton lexicon, the idea of chance is absent, as it has been absent from the world of all children and all primitive peoples. In the presence, then, of this man's writings, I am drawn into a religion of possession.

Each story, each vision in this book, is a throw of the dice. The act of reading makes me a gambler. The role of gambler is a familiar one to me and I have, as a consequence, acquired familiar expectations, predictable compulsions based on chance, a comfortable part of my reality.

But with each of these stories, with each throw of the dice, I, the reader, the gambler trapped in a changing reality, feel in the service of an alien power. This then is a dangerous realm for the reader, the gambler, to enter.

For with this book, we risk the dangerous power of genius —of one who can construct a universe within the skull, to rival the real. And it is a universe, we are sternly cautioned, in "The Bleeding Man" and in other stories herein, that exists, in desperation, without polite, civilized limits. For we are told, are we not, IF ALL ELSE FAILS, WE CAN WHIP THE HORSE'S EYES AND MAKE HIM CRY AND SLEEP!

Jorge Luis Borges, 1976

IF ALL ELSE FAILS . . .

SATURDAY NIGHT AT THE WHITE WOMAN WATCHING HOLE

We was in there, a place so posh they served old jokes in stirrup cups. Him out of prison, me studying for it. Both Cherokee kazoo birds, getting high in high society, leaping up at the cocktail and catching flies while the air whistled through our kazoo sides.

Yeah, we got noticed. I think, patronwise, they was more thinking of having, you know, a full course of orchestra or opera, maybe ballet watchers under glass. Anything but Turquoise Ties.

You tell us why we were eating out, we wouldn't know. We were better at biting the dust than dining out. We shouldn't have been there, but all the girls we knew walked sideways and we wanted to see one that knew how to sit down straight without surprising anybody.

The waiter, with a coat sharp enough to slice Puerto Ricans, is hovering around us dangerously, like a tree afraid of losing its leaves. He's making us as nervous as we are making him. We can't take it much more. It's worse than waiting for a flood to recede. We were all ready to go when she came in.

Her. She sat down so straight the chair barked. All the waiters fell down, covered with dirt, when they saw her. To look at her was to feel unzipped in public. Her eyes looked like they would never tell you about it either. She moved

like a sedate funeral oration, no wasted motion. She had
learned to arch her carefully pruned eyebrows at Wimble-
don. Just looking, you knew she had a Billie Jean King
handshake and a Bobby Riggs foreplay. You could talk
about her but never quite touch her. She was the fifth ace in
a third-wheel deck. Too much.

"Wouldn't you like to run your train over that?" he says
and I am thinking I guess I would.

"She could get your wheels really wet." Yeah. He's thinking he would like it too. She's the woman hardhats aren't allowed to have.

No good being rich unless you know how to wear it. She
wore it good. Clothes arranged by cyclotron and the work of
ten thousand generations of sleepless peasants, stitching
their lives away into the hem of the perfect garment. She
had a cigarette-lighting routine with the gold case and ta-
pered, contoured lighter that said, TOULOUSE LAUTREC
SLEPT HERE BUT ONLY ONCE. She was just about too
dainty to touch, all shot full of arts and crafts and Manhat-
tan Uptown. A narrow face but beautiful if you read
women's magazines and believed what you read. Refined,
cultured, pottie trained by the proper schools and the
proper family. Closest she ever got to dirt was flying over
Pennsylvania in a jet.

Even our waiter ducked away because she came in like
an event and stuck out like a horizon. Everybody rushed to
ride off into her sunset. Her voice, ordering with a nun's for-
bidden-life quality, smooth, repressed syllables, words that
haven't lived until she utters them. The waiter bobs up and
down in front of her as if she were about to hand him a
hand grenade with her fragrance on it.

She was so very, very good at being her. Everything
about her was so exceedingly. Her perfectly formed feet
were exceedingly. Her cultured hands, Vassar nose, Jamaica

Midnight eyes, slow drizzle in them, maybe sexual. Everything about her was so very exceedingly . . . something.

Her waiter, once ours, galloped away like a tame dog to fetch a pair of slippers. She said thank you so graciously, the waiter's hands perspired.

"I was thinking, scratching my prison mentality for wormy thoughts and it occurs to me, we oughta look around for a camera. Or maybe armed guards. I don't think we should be allowed to look at her without a license. She's the Royal Crown Jewels with legs," he says.

"I gotta know her," I said. "She's the kind of woman who can have rubber balls for breasts and still be forgiven. I wanna meet her."

He looks at me the wrong way through the wrong end of his drink. "Are you out of your mind? You could get arrested for rape for touching her used napkins! She wouldn't touch you with a ten-foot Indian agent." He can't believe I said that. He sticks his nose in his drink and blows bubbles derisively. He doesn't think I am serious.

"No. Really. I have to try to talk to her, shake her hand, knee her accidentally in the tail, something. Just so I can say I did it once. I want to comprehend her. I want to understand her enough to lose my fascination for it."

"Huh? You're drunk." Yeah. He's right. I'm drunk. Everyone is, one way or another.

"Man, just between you and me and the rodeo circuit, I want to teach her how to make her belly button laugh and cry."

He waves his arms, disgusted. "She'll pull a tear-gas gun out of her lap and blow your eyes out the back of your head," he said. He's really disgusted. "Course, I could be wrong; New York City women may wear them in the higher hair. Maybe she'll pull it out of her armpit. Blow your face off anyway."

The waiter comes out in a one-man procession and gives

birth to a dietetic salad which he puts in front of her, hoping she will take it to her breast and nurse it. She blinks once and he jumps away like he is afraid his hands will give birth to another one.

"I wonder what she does for a living."

That expression of disgust again. I am making him consistent. "You're stupid. Hell, she just lives and everybody else does for her. Forget her, she's out of our laps. Let's go someplace else. Goddamn waiter can shove this place! The food's probably lousy here anyway. None of the truck drivers eat here."

He gets up to leave, the prison suit they gave him, tight around the shoulders. I'm still sitting there, looking.

"You go ahead. I'm going to follow her."

He just kind of folds up. Can't keep other people from killing themselves, his only flaw. Runs for cover, waits till the blood gets dry. Always says, I told you so. He hands me the bill, six drinks, $22.50, with cover charge. Heads out the door with his tail up, a girl's address on Twenty-sixth Street in his pocket. Cuts a fine figure but a little too close.

I am left alone, subdivided, and the waiter is one-half happy. Nods at me curtly, what you call a subtle hint. He's hovering around me again, strafing the table with meaningful looks. Reminds me of a traffic controller at a bordello. I pick up the bill, the not-so-subtle hint of a little bit ago. Wave it at the waiter. He's on the way before I even touch it.

A blur where the money changes hands, the door opens, and I am out on the street. Waiter at the door sweeping invisible moccasin marks from the entranceway carpet.

Ten minutes, fifteen. I'm waiting. The girl's made out of imported china. Has vintage wine in her blood. Eats slowly, pondering every bite through an opera-glass coating on her tongue.

She must be finished by now, paying for the meal by

touch of hands only, maybe just a superior look. Maybe they pay her to come in and lift the funeral off the place. Maybe.

The door glides open and out she comes. Striding, ducking her head at an invisible doorman. Moves to the street, looks for taxicabs. The wrong time of day. Two stop at once, one flipping its sign over to read on duty. She bows graciously at them both. Gets into the first one, exchanges diplomatic smile with other driver, who waves back at her, hides his loss.

While she's getting into the first one, I grab the second. I tell the cabbie, "Follow that cab."

He turns around and gives me one hell of a look. "Goddamn tourist" is what he says under his breath, and flips the meter on. Me, I don't care how demented he thinks I am, I just want to see her house, just the outside of the mansion. Maybe urinate on some of her landscaping. Assault the butler. Follow the fox to ground. Something.

Is that girl real? She's too perfect. Can't imagine her going to the bathroom. She just holds it, looks apologetic, shrugs it off casually. Or hires a Frenchman to do it. I have to see where she lives like a climber goes for Mount Everest, because it's there. Because it's there and everything sane says I'm not supposed to be.

The cab ride is forever, within two bucks of all the money I have. Paid the cabbie off a block behind her. Location, an ugly brownstone building in a bad section. Am a lot puzzled. She couldn't live here, must be slumming.

She walked to the front door, didn't knock, just opened and walked in. Had a kind of casual familiarity with the place. An everyday look on her face, the kind of expression a movie queen uses playing gin rummy between takes with two people from a cast of thousands. Slumming.

I got in front of the house, couldn't believe she was inside. Had to follow, probably the dump was a secret hideout of ambassadors of state. I open the door and I'm in. It's an en-

tranceway, a long hall, and she is just disappearing out of
sight into the last room at the end. No noise anywhere. The
building is empty.

I don't know what I am doing but I do it. This building
should be condemned. Holes in the floor, plaster giving in to
gravity. I creep up the hallway, wondering exactly what I'm
trying to prove.

A rat runs along the edge of the hall. It's the kind of
building rats would abandon. I move farther along down the
hallway. The door to the room she has entered is lightly ajar.
It's dark in there. Nothing to see. Time to get out of there,
but then there I am, down on my haunches, pushing on the
door ever so slightly, widening the crack a tiny fraction. I
hear a scratching sound.

She's lighting a candle, a dim thing, then another and another. Her back is to me. The room is unfurnished, littered
with old rags and soiled newspapers, wallpaper hanging in
tattering banners down the walls. Ceiling probably held together with flyspecks.

I can't see what she's doing. Something is on the floor and
she's bent over it, her shadow covers it, can't make it out in
the dark. She's in the corner, bent over awkwardly, using
some kind of tool.

Hunting for buried treasure, digging up the floor? No,
there's something above the floor, can't make it out. Eyes
have to adjust. The candles are arranged around her on the
floor. She raises something over her head like a club, metal
and narrow, curved, swings and there is a thud, a tearing
sound.

She is tearing at something, jerking her arms toward her.
Gouging. Working at it furiously. Something very wrong
here, in a cocktail dress. My eyes strain, fascinated. She
turns around a little and I can see over one of her shoulders.

It's a corpse.

She moves a candle closer and moves off to one side. I can see it clearly now. The body of a man.

The corpse is stretched out on his back, chest slit from side to side, torn apart from chin to neck. His torn shirt lies across his outstretched arms. There is blood and I can see how careful she is with her dress because of it. She bends over daintily to get at him. She has a warehouseman's hook, long, curved, and with it, she is tearing away at his entrails. Slamming the curved point of the hook into the thorax, tearing out ribs and lungs, red flesh.

She croons softly, rocking on her heels, and I am now afraid she'll see me. Time to leave but I am as fascinated by her as she is with the corpse. A heartbeat rhythm. Stab and rip, stab and rip. There is a machine quality, a sexual essence to her movements. Total concentration.

She turns around more, her hook fouled with visceral material and I see her eyes. In them, the same preoccupation with opera, charities, modern dance. She wipes the hook against the corpse's thigh and looks up at the door, unsurprised.

I am startled, jerk forward, bump against the door and it swings open with a loud creak. She stops with the hook, poised over the body. She stares at me. I don't know what to do, when to run. She makes no move to threaten me.

She turns and plunges the hook into the head of the corpse, a grand, theatrical gesture. The hook bites in, tears out an eye. She looks back at me to see if I am watching. I am. I'm too frozen to do otherwise. The hook goes up and down, rips through the side of the man's face. She stops again, her stare at me has changed, taken on a new meaning. She now expects something out of me.

I couldn't leave, couldn't turn away until I gave it to her. She had some kind of hold over me. Some power. The hook bites the other eye, rips it out. And then I know. I know what she wants, what she asks of me.

I can understand her well enough now to be no longer fascinated by it. I had seen the carefully planned woman, a woman made, not born. The bone-china lady, the society bird of the carefully planned dress. She expected no more out of me than she expected out of the corpse.

I stood up slowly, straightening the knees for easy flight. I knew then, even before she smiled graciously.

I put my hands together and applauded.

ALL MY STATUES
HAVE STONE WINGS

I wanted to write this letter and mail it to you because you don't live here anymore. I wanted to tell you that it was the wind, that kind of wind between men and women that drives the fishbones out of fish. The angry skeleton falls out and the fish won't swim anymore. It was that kind of wind. This is that kind of letter. The wind will mail it for me.

We met at the museum. I was ethnic art; you were abstraction. I was a stranger to you but I had seen you many times before. I had seen you posed in every possible camera angle in every foreign film that ever played. Cameras explored your face; you were a blond-haired planet, no, a sun and all the world revolved around you. You were the enormous cosmic empty bottle into which the teeming masses would empty themselves trying to fill you. Your eyes were blue and I walked over to you. I told you I thought your forehead was paradise between two light bulbs. You smiled and nodded weary agreement. You had heard it all before.

You were dressed in peaches, halved with light syrup, and I wore my penitentiary suit. My suit was made of license plates with the name of the state misspelled. I was naked. Naked but I wore a hat, that argued a personal style.

Your artwork hung next to me in the art gallery. I was my own artwork. Your exhibit consisted of green canvasses painted blue and blue canvasses painted green. You had studied in France, Paris, and I had studied in Quentin, San.

The art competition was fierce. The judges lingered at your exhibit long enough to raise your expectations. Had you painted a blue canvas blue and a green one green, you might have won. That's what the judges said as they passed you by.

I didn't win either. My exhibit consisted of me walking barefoot through broken glass attired only in a somber black hat. The bright red splashes of blood on the floor excited the judges. I might have won but like a fool, when one of the judges asked me what were the chances of my bleeding to death, I admitted that the possibility was slight. The judges walked away muttering about artistic insincerity.

You sought me out, feeling that the trip to Paris had somehow been wasted, and had a good cry on my shoulder. I wheezed sympathetically and played a cello in my throat. I held you in one hand and got dressed with the other. While you helped me wrap up my bleeding feet, you fell in love with me. It happened very suddenly. I took off my hat and my braids tumbled past my shoulders. Your blue eyes made slot-machine motions. I slipped the shirt over my shoulders and put the hat back on. During that movement you fell in love with me. I, in turn, let you pay the rent.

You loved the color of my skin and the eagles in my eyes. Together our bodies played off-Broadway, and like cars that crouched in the soft tar of your highways, our hearts exploded metallically in your furnished room, eighty-five dollars a month, no pets. We held hands and sat bumper to bumper in the dark.

You teased me with your camera-perfect face. You made my heart explode like the slugs in slots between coin-operated buildings. You dispensed tender moments in measured portions. You were experienced in delight. You had slept with policemen.

You gave me the New York City tour and you made talking through your nose sound sophisticated. You paraded me before your friends. They harvested me, they touched my bow hand, they scooped me up with broken glass. I had to endlessly explain wigwams and how to fall off horses. I felt the hum of their social motors making expeditions through the reservation of my heart.

We went to all the parties. We played charades. I always took the parts that no one could guess. I pretended to be the inside of a concentration camp. At masquerades, I went disguised as a human being. Once I won a prize for best costume. I was dressed as the INVISIBLE MAN.

We went to a party on Halloween night. You spent the entire evening trying to seduce a *black* football player. He passed out drunk in front of you like a period at the end of a sentence. You were enraged. Your roommate in college, Sylvia something or other, had slept with one once. I couldn't remember if you wanted to try it because Sylvia had liked it or because she hadn't.

I spent a lot of time in a corner, trying not to get cornered. One of your friends tried to engage me in conversation. She said, "My television said something interesting yesterday."

"I don't want to tell you any jokes, but the word antelope loses its meaning when clothed in a tuxedo," I said, hoping to end the conversation.

Your friend began an elaborate set of gestures, communicating a comic strip. She touched her teeth with her painted nails. It reminded me of my grandfather who always advised, Look for signs and omens. It reminded me of my grandfather who died humming all the songs he had kept silent because there was no one left to sing them to. We buried him in the ground like a dead bee in a window box.

Your friend began another conversation with the rest of her body. "I'm afraid my shoes are awfully late," she confided, "but I'm sure you'll forgive me if I lean against your body. The wind may push me over on top of you any minute. Incidentally, have you been to the theater and did I take your ticket?"

She stood so close to me, her body almost hid the room. Through the angles under her arms, I saw a line forming behind her. I sensed a system of sisterhood. She recognized me from somewhere. As if she had known me, as if I had been her lover once in the dark and had brought her sedatives.

Then you came back and reclaimed me from the sandbar where they served eggrolls along the conversational river. All your friends kissed me good-bye. They said they were sorry to hear that my arms could not be cut off for souvenirs. You whirled me out the door and we walked away from the party.

As we strolled past the antiwoodpecker factories of New York, you were beginning to think of me in artistic terms. I could see it in your face. You were planning my next exhibit and I could see it take shape along the cliff of your face, spreading upward like a glacier to your eyes.

When you got an idea it came to you slowly, and I could see it coming for years, like a poet with promise or a street improvement. I was your ship in a bottle and you kept stuffing messages into me. You had missed out on the black football player but you were flexible. You told me that you were going to take me home to meet your parents.

In the next breath, you offered me a warrant for my arrest in the form of a marriage proposal. I agreed because my vocabulary was limited. Besides, you paid the rent, eighty-five a month, no pets.

The next morning, you began dressing me for the journey. You made me wear the moccasins that were too tight and put plastic bead chokers around my neck. You made me wear the medicine bag you bought on sale at Macy's. You were specially insistent that I look as much like the me of me that was me.

On the drive over, as your car swerved through the back streets you once cruised in high school, I tried to hide in your shoulder. I, being culturally shy, sought soft asylum but your arms were busy driving. There was no place for me to hide. You were filled with a grim determination that made you seem like a scientist counting drops of blood in the teeming cells of a corpse.

You were assaulting the temple. I was your blasphemy. Your parents were the high priests. And we went to see where they worshiped.

Your father was in the backyard, aggravating crabgrass. The house looked like a house. It sat in an endless row of houses. All of those houses looked like houses too. Your mother came to the door to meet us and she looked like your mother.

She screamed with delight when she saw you. She bent over backward to smile at me and the smile ricocheted off the floor. She yelled like a football coach and your father, perhaps thinking the worst, came running into the house, still carrying his garden trowel.

How many years since they saw you last, I never knew; but your father threw his arms around you and would have picked you up like a little girl his arms once held if you hadn't pushed him away. Their bones were frail and their eyes filled deeply with tears. Their eyes were like tiny music boxes, spilling each tear like a musical note.

They swept us into the living room, cutting the air in front of our path with quick, surprised gestures. The way they looked at you was the way people in family albums look, camera shy, frozen at some awkward moment and pose, in front of a world that moves somewhere outside the frame of the photograph.

You steered me ahead of you like a shield, aiming me like

a weapon at the look in their eyes that remembered a little girl with yellow hair and blue eyes. You held me up against them and you said, "This is the man I am going to marry."

And your father was so glad to see you, he shook my hand and tried very hard to listen closely enough to catch my name. Your mother moved her lips together in a tight line and then smiled. She pulled me to her and hugged me like her arms ached.

When she let me go, my fingers had nowhere to go on the ends of my hands and I flopped loosely before them, smiling like an idiot, bobbing my head up and down for conversational apples.

Your mother whirled you away to show you something that existed only as an excuse to talk to you alone. Your father smiled at me fearfully. His eyes studied my accessories. The silence grew between us until suddenly as if a spring had snapped, he began speaking in rapid-fire sentences, spitting out thoughts like links of varnished sausages. We rapidly discovered that we could talk about anything but each other.

My answers were as vague and as agreeable as his questions. Your mother appeared at the doorway and called him away. Your father excused himself and went into the kitchen with a glassy look on his face.

I sat there uncomfortably and couldn't help overhearing you arguing with them. You were yelling, using phrases like social imperative, genetic-upgrading, cross-cultural reinforcement, and rear-end alignment. Your parents spoke not a word. You mistook this silence flowing within them as disapproval and your voice rose in pitch and became triumphant. You sensed their untutored dissent and it spurred you on. Your lecture was footnoted with swear words that once entertained troopships. You sensed victory in sweet denial.

But they took you by the arm, one on each side, and together, the three of you, the two of them silent, you triumphant in martyrdom, came toward me.

Your father put his hand on my shoulder and looked me in the eye. He said, "If my daughter loves you and wants to marry you, then we welcome you into the family."

That was the last time I ever saw you. Your parents approved of me and you never forgave them. You never came back to the apartment to pick up your things. Your father called me twice to see how we were doing. Maybe he called again after that but I don't know. I had to leave when the rent came due.

I went back to the museum where I first met you. I searched all the abstractions for you. I thought I saw you in the classical period. Just a glimpse but when I got closer it was only a stone woman a long-dead Greek had given wings. I touched the statue's marble face and let my fingers scrape the smooth surface of the wings.

The statue had your face. It had your marble eyes. I climbed across the rope barrier and stood beneath your stone wings. The shadow of your wings fell across my face like a cold satellite in the sky.

I climbed up the stone folds of your garments and looked into your cold eyes. I saw it in your eyes, a song, a martyr's song that said, "The fire next time." You never gave up. Those cold eyes of yours were out there somewhere, looking for a Negro. Looking for a Negro to tuck under your stone wing. With any luck, an ugly one.

And all my statues have stone wings.

TEN TIMES YOUR FINGERS
AND DOUBLE YOUR TOES

It was black, black, and he turn all ways like a stuck snake and people all around saying they ain't have no work. It came for him that six week go by and he ain't working and he just saying hell about it all over.

He owe everybody. He is bird naked and they knows it. He got a dime for the white trader and ten dollars for the old man who works the chin game on the next tourist who comes round the bend. And, too, he owe ten-dollar credits to old man name Backet 'cause it caught up with him and the last time he went there Backet showed him how to go out the same door he come in, only faster.

"You son of bitch!" yells Stonecloud, sitting down like poleaxed ballerina in the street. "You could have waited till the tourist season! You know I'm good for it, you old product of stale dog heat!"

But Backet, he remember flush time last year but it don't make him soft. And he don't give him nothing to drink and tell him to go out and die like the dog he is or pay.

This put the by god fix on Stonecloud 'cause he hungry and dirty, and looking all ways up and down, he don't see nothing to come. His shoe got a big hole in it like it laughing at him and the cold rain is chilling him on the body like a reptile dream.

"Lousy head hunker! I rich as hell in tourist season!" Spitting old language of sparks and grumbling, he got up and began walking down the street. Up above, with him not even having to look, he knows is the sky and it is being all wrong and the season is six maybe seven week yet. And he know from empty pocket to empty pocket it no use to go down to the port and wait for no ships to come. The charter ships with the green people wouldn't be coming roaring out of the sky no way until the rains be got to stop. He know that like a toothache on a callus on his soul. It such a hungry.

"That Backet, he wait till I rich. Come tourists, I biscuit and gravy rich. I am virtue of Cadillac, full four-wheeled and pockct heavy. Come tourists, I rich. I dog bark on his old man, Backet and business." And he mutter to himself all time think the dog will be on the other roof like or not when he rich.

As he walking on down the street all time disgusted the sky seeing him so fly unzipped in the attitude, come pouring out rain like eternal vigilance. It raining so hard it bounce hitting down.

"Oh lousy of all!" moan Stonecloud feeling the bounce bounce of rain seeping down into his wet underbeing. Nothing but for to keep on walking on past the stores, keeping the sharp eye for someone who owes him something. But he find no one and it rain all over and his shoe laughingly taking in water like an old-time-fashion tax collection.

He stop in front of a newsstand to duck under the awning and get out of the wet but government boy with plastic straw dangling out of liquid concentrate of beefsteak dangling out of shirt pocket come banging up to the counter like a angry hornet. He drop a handful of newstapes on counter and gives with the eye like he asking maybe are you selling tickets to the RESURRECTION already. And government boy begin yelling as he is government, "Hey, you! This ain't no flophouse!"

So what happen is Stonecloud shout right back and scorch

air with hot language and, 'cause he proud, he take a credit
out of his pocket. It is his lucky credit he won in a tumbling
game that time he had many year ago, when he had chance
to win that funny boy in the three-day game in Aztol's garage. He chicken out and refuse to bet last credit and old
Aztol, who all time thinking the pretty boy is woman as is
all players but old Hawkfoot who put up same for stake, win
bet and funny boy, much to roar of roars when he find out
he been tacked up in sun and let to dry. So ever after, as he
had had old Aztol beat, he had kept lucky credit as protection against funny boys. So now he take lucky credit and
smash it, and protection it provide, on counter like it being a
fly to get smashed. And he grab up a newstape and walk
away with back up like a picket fence and head held high.

Course he get out of sight of newsstand and government
boy, he curse the saints of painted donkeys and the eggs of
their grandmothers and go all tight in face on account he
don't have no newstape reader, so newstape is worth having
like hickey from poison snake. So he pitch newstape into
street when he is sure someone is looking at his extra extrav-
agance, and newstape it get sucked up into rotors of a pie
wagon and goes into shreds. All which reminds him he is
hungry enough to eat cookbook and he hit head like a
drunken burglar who has shut jimmied wall safe on his shoe-
laces.

He look and he look into his memory and he can't remember even one name of who owes him something. He
spend so much time try to forget who he owe money to himself that he forget if anybody owe him.

So he stop in front of a travel agency and drip rain and go
to looking in at the moving window pictures. All the planets
are there in pictures with edges. Every picture has smiling
green people or some kind of other color people he don't
even know name of, not mattering to him much, though, as
once you see one kind of color people they all look pretty

much alike. All these smiling people sitting around and running and jumping and kidding around in the bushes which are placed just so, so little kids can't come see who or how they are kidding around. No worry on their faces and all the time acting like a nest of ants in a sugarbowl. He think they tell each other too many jokes or been all hit in the head too many times as he is surprised to see so much kidding around in one place. He chuckle in the neck and think wicked that they have all caught the old IT in the middle and limp bow-legged, and it go up and make oatmeal with lumps of their brains. But still they eat all the time and dance and kid each other like it won't fall off from too much kidding around and it is all hell depressing.

And it all disgust him and he go down the street collecting a lake from his shoe comedy routine, flap, slosh, flap, slosh, all the much hotter than before. He is feeling by now as hot as nine wicked cats in a dark room.

Now Stonecloud never steal. He gamble. He play loose with an ace. He drink like a parched horse, he chase women when he got enough money to slow them down. He never steal. He never catch a woman who don't want caught and he never steal.

So he go by a storeful of shoes and he almost break a leg trying to walk past it by standing still. He look through the front window like a guilty cat with feathers on his breath. He catch himself on the throat and pull himself away and push himself on down the street, but his legs not convinced and he know it.

The first step away from store he takes he hit a puddle and he feel the splash through his shoe clear to his lap. It is rain, cold rain like a funny boy's kisses, and his feet getting cold numb from hip on down.

So he suck in his bird-feather breath and he spin around like gravity pulling down an old sock and is pulled back in front of the store windowful of shoes and burn slowly. All the time he is thinking he could be beautiful from the feet up.

The automatic clerk is hunched on a table like somebody's old appendix operation. His eyebulbs are unlit and his speaking crack dangles open like a bear snore. Stonecloud pop goes the weasel his eyes at the temptation. There is sign on robot clerk showing how busy like a buried coffin is shoe store. The sign say: FOR SERVICE, PLEASE ACTIVATE SWITCH 3 ON FRONT OF ROBO-CLERK. THANK YOU.

The store was all over shoes. It look like place where all old shoemakers go to die, dropping shoes like elephant tusks where they fall. It is the shoe-elephant graveyard.

Stonecloud standing out there like an apology, standing there touching the bottom of his pockets and he sees shoes, old and new and black and blue. And he thinks of them unguiltily in three-part harmony. He couldn't even count all the shoes. He look like eagle eyestrain is having him popeyed and he thinking all time, "They got them. So many. Ten times my fingers and double my toes. Oh lousy of all! And I stand with toes taking swimming lesson."

So he pretend he don't recognize himself and he slip quietly through the front door like a dumb-and-deaf act at the tourist circus. He looks at robot clerk with the smile of unprincipled beauty and tiptoes around him ever lightly. And Stonecloud he look up at thief catching close-circuit TV camera and then down at monitor beside robo-clerk and it give him a laugh. The TV monitor on the blitz and show being on is not being interior of store at all but old-time rerun of *I Lust For Lucy*. All of which is all more perfect safe. Then he gets right up next to clerk and does the jackhammer staccato shuffle and flap-slosh dance for the robot clerk's ears only. But the robot clerk is the sleeping beauty only activated by the kiss of a handsome priss on the activating switch. As soon as Stonecloud sees he had got no applause and there be no audience, he was knowing it was safe as breathing. So he squirt around like a marshmallow in the soup. He look here and he look here and he fussy as old men needing prunes.

First he latch on to a black pair fit for a king. He try them on and they fit like royalty on people. He yelps at tight squeeze, takes shoes off, and dumps them in the garbage can. He keep looking.

Then he find a pair that are all perfect. He put them on and leave his old pair of holes beside the robot clerk. Stonecloud nods friendly like at the clerk who look like activating mechanism of white liberal freedom fighter. And then like a ghostly gift giver he walks out of the store, like he bought something. Stonecloud act like it too and keeps going away.

And it hit him suddenly; it was hell easy. Stonecloud was hit, as he had not known it as hell easy as even telling a lie in public office. But in three-part harmony, all surrounded, all piled high and so many, more than ten times his fingers and double his toes, it was hell easy.

Stonecloud spring down the street bouncing on his new shoes like a basketball. He get feeling like old self again, and he remembers how all the time all the women used to tongue snap when he come bounce with credits in one hand and fancy suit all slicked up like a crooked dog tied sideways. Didn't they just snap tongue when he rode high in tourist time. Good remembering, his feet unswimming, all smiling, somewhat bouncing all went to the cleaner's when his stomach kicked him in the back remembering him he was hungry as a perpetual-motion stomach-pump machine.

Wouldn't he go to bite something or, hungry as is, somebody? He mad for food and that make him think of mostly somewhat-drinking-to-stupidness Aztol and his garage with the fruit locker full of obsolescent oranges and too-long-remembered bananas. Even rotten as is make him water all over the mouth and tongue hum like piano-tuner attachment. So he bounce twice for extra traction and then he making like an arthritic fire engine and scoot scoot scoot through the ever-bouncing rain like a winded frog.

Aztol was sitting in a chair in his garage talking to his dog which he got in trade for the funny boy he won in a tumbling game. The dog was asleep as it wasn't much of a dog on account you can't expect no time to get an undamaged one for a funny boy, and this was nobody's noise of an exception. Most he was bent up and lean forward when he walk, like he trying to see down the front of some hyperventilating midget lady's dress which there was not many of on hand. Aztol was tongue flapping like big-time brag stuff about time when the old Tourist Center burn down during party. Aztol was trying remember if was himself set fire or what. He couldn't remember so good.

Stonecloud bounce in like something crawled off breakfast cereal box.

Aztol look up and think he see a drowned bird and is smelling maybe a long dead one. Aztol roll up his lips like a soggy cracker.

"What about ten credits owed me? What? What? What?"

The smile on Stonecloud's face sail to edge and fall off the world.

"Oh the horse!" he curse. "You knowing I good for it when all time of season come!"

Aztol drop eyes like a plum bob and down looking he see new shoes, and eyes light up like free pinball game. It makes him hot. He roll a nasty thought in his head. "Twenty-five credit brick on the hooves!" He roar like a hydroelectric plant. "Twenty-five credit and got no money for old guy Aztol! Who who you?"

Stonecloud look hungry at fruit locker and see a picture of a fruit locker standing in its place. He groan as he realize art imitate life but get screwed in here and now. Name being pretty to look at but doing nothing to stomach, he sigh and flap arms like wings of gilded rooster, mating with lesser angel.

Says he, mouth unwatering, "I flew them from captivity."

"You steal! Not pay! Steal?" Aztol look stomach kicked.

"Broke. Had to. Wave my knees in the trees if I lie. Broke," said Stonecloud, dropping his arms in a bowling ball throwing motion.

"Can you not wait for tourist?" asked Aztol.

"Plant me drowned from bottom up if waited six weeks. Old shoes holes with laces. Had to. Had to." Stonecloud shrugged, dripping rain for emphasis.

"You a disgrace being Indian," grunted Aztol. "Boost shoes like common thief."

"Well all same, I had to—"

"You disgrace," cut in Aztol. "Going go to jail a disgrace for measly shoes look like overenlarged rabbit pellets with grooves anyway. I ashamed to call you Indian. Gonna steal, boost truck of whiskey! What you want known as, champion bird's-nest ransacker?"

Stonecloud roll back head and laugh kiff-fiff as it hits him like first false pregnancy of spring. Always a good joke.

Aztol scratch his unwoven chin hair, eye Stonecloud try to grind giggle to halt.

"You know you could have moneys if wanted. From tourist," say Aztol, eye winking at himself in moderation. Aztol smirked, effect knowing of this statement, smirked more even as he be self-freshening.

Stonecloud leap forward like liberated bosom bounce, news catching to face and sticking there like memory of snout kick from unprincipled mule. He all sudden more eyes and ears than sixteen dancing monkeys in the house of mirrors.

"What? What?" he shout, making frantic slot-machine motions with his chin.

Aztol smug, smiled like uncorked leper cutting loose from his first fallen finger. He look bored of whole thing. He knuckle crack as an infuriation and pronounced delay of game.

"What? What?" Jumping up like flopped fish and enunciating like a yodeling moose echo, goes Stonecloud. "What?"

Aztol yawn and look like maybe he curl up and sleep. He stop act when Stonecloud look like he going to go for jugular like smell of fish rising to ceiling. This all too solid inevitable, and Aztol take a tuck in his intentions, having met the experience they be aimed for, finding as always, room for improvement, as loving one's neighbor was same sandwich, but pickle difference being on when husband get home. Aztol know how much market can take. He ease off gracefully like senility in shock absorbers.

"Tourist coming today," quick says Aztol in self-deference. "Didn't you be knowing this?"

Stonecloud bounce shoes twice, only once touching ground. "Oh the horse!" he curse and he go like two truck-drivers driving the same truck.

"I think shoes stink!" yells Aztol, but Stonecloud is moving at twice the speed of leaf rustle in empty swimming pool and is too far gone to hear.

Stonecloud pounds up to Tourist Center, gasping like carelessly calibrated alligator in vacuum. Sure as goats have the smell of style that asks for distance, a ship was down. He run like possession, perhaps Rebecca of Sunnybrook Farm, the demon that got him. He runs on both legs and leaps through the big doors like imitation of last sardine getting into can. He sees the green ones scattered all around, most occupied, and he hears screams of guns and bark of the dying. He snatch gun from wall brackets with lend-lease frenzy, check if loaded, and race away to get tourist for all gone.

He found her standing in one of the tourist sun room. She look proper horrify when she see him come bounce with gun. She even scream like soprano-air-raid siren. It is goose-bump delicious, he know. She sink her scream to buzz-saw roar, very small horsepowers.

He aim gun and hesitate as always. The thrill of kill was in the shrill. He wait for full-lung expansion and full eyepop and complete first parachute jump, no I-take-it-back syndrome after you already too far down to walk back up. She is ready. He is ready.

He look at her close. She short, maybe twenty hands high, green scale on body, sharp pointed fingers that made good drink stirring rods, if proper dry. She got vents each side of face for breathing and air conditioning, factory air. Other accessories, sharp bony ridge down center of narrow face, and best, white-sidewall clenched knuckles. She regard him with two lidless headlight of horror.

He aim, thinking of food, new clothes, all them women gonna snap tongue at him, and Philadelphia. He always have it in for Philadelphia. The gun screamed its own language, the bullet hit her big culture shock in chest, and she fell over backwards like stacked deck. She still screaming, getting all out of it she can.

The tourist alarm rang. Stonecloud sit down to wait. The fix it or forget it machine roll in, and scoop up body, also give floor wash and wax job and count cracks in ceiling. It keep busy. Help take mind off tourists. They all pain in processor. Machine start processing, adding short pithy message on cellular-level sponsor by CITIZENS FOR DECENT LITERATURE.

It take time, and Stonecloud, he impatient as lamppost-leaning girl in forty day and forty night of rain. So he have plenty time to think. He think first he going to make big-time cash deposit to restaurant first, so time he hungry all he do is walk in, sit down, and eat like stupidness. He all for stupidness; go easy on the eggs and no Philadelphia. He always have it in for Philadelphia.

Then next he going to head to toe, clothes to eyepop women and make all go tongue snap. And he thinking how he is going to buy and sell everyone and then he feel like dance and that when he notice remembering his shoes. He look down at feet. He not dance.

Stonecloud sitting there in marble-shooter position number seven, and then there is this tapping on his shoulder like touch of gay sparrow. Stonecloud look up and see white-man tourist with brown socks and checkered pants.

"Isn't this something! Isn't this just something!" says the tourist, says this white-man tourist bumping cameras off his chest.

"Isn't?" ask Stonecloud.

"Me and the Mrs. drove up from Philadelphia to see some of these aliens. I tell you this, this is really something!"

"Well, suck an old dog," say Stonecloud, "is nothing to covet outhouses over!"

The tourist guy is bouncing around, snapping snapshots, yelling off somewhere for someone named Gladys and snap snap snap, pictures of sky and knees and Stonecloud and ground and mostly shots of alien female in clutches of fix it or forget it machine.

"Don't you just think it is incredible, I mean, they come all the way here, I mean, all the way to Earth, pay to come here, pay to get shot. I mean, what a bunch of alien freaks! I mean, ain't it incredible! Isn't that truly unbelievable?"

Stonecloud pinch up his face in gesture of disgust and facial snarl of overfamiliarity, and he say nothing like vacuum cleaner doing his tongue.

"She's gonna come out of the machine soon!" squeals the

tourist excitedly. "Oh Jesus! I'm out of film. What a Goddamn time to run out of . . . Gladys! Gladys!"

"Christopher Columbus was absolute nut tourist too!
Goddamn crazy man! He not know horses about camera or
good guns, but he have crotch disease go like last souvenirs
before the desert," say Stonecloud. "Wish to groundhog we
could have . . ."

The white tourist go run off yelling for Gladys and film,
and Stonecloud relieved to see him go as would be to wake
up in morning and find he not in Philadelphia. Stonecloud
all time thinking how tourist season is get too big to ride
sidesaddle as now tourists are coming to see tourists being
tourists. Pretty soon be shooting himself as tourist, think
Stonecloud.

Fix it or forget it machine is taking one forever. Just as
Stonecloud getting ready to bite down on impatience so
hard he give gums flesh wounds, along come white woman;
must be Gladys 'cause she got film cartridges in one hand
and is dressed up looking like sack of concrete and liquid
laundry detergent container. She rumpled like milk sitting
too long on radiator.

"Where is the aliens? Where is the freaks? Where is
Frank?" she say, sputtering like outboard motor, put put
put.

"Where is . . . ?"

She is starting again and Stonecloud, by god, fed up with
whole donkey. No where is said he got to feel like inside of
doughnut for two sets of tourist. He jumps at her and leers at
her and waves gun in her face, and she look at him like she
in a hurry and he is double-parked in her space.

She ignore him complete as she hears husband or maybe
wild hog with stomach gas yelling for film somewhere off
somewhere. She spin off and leave Stonecloud feeling like
phallic cannon in civil-war exhibit, erected no less.

Then alien come out of machine, she all shiny like fuzz on

newborn peach. She smell like ghost of a chance in the second race before the man with the shovel comes out on the track. She look like second honeymoon making same old mistakes.

Machine burp her and she stand up and step out of machine. She walk over to him, reaching into her shoulder pouch. She open mouth, she smile, show sharp-pointed teeth. This is gratitude.

"It was beautiful! It was wonderful!" she say.

Stonecloud smile like carnival employee winning teddy bear just next door. He not know what to say. He never know.

"The savagery, the pain! Exquisite!" she said, and she shake with pleasure like flagellating blender and hug herself like wraparound sunglasses.

Stonecloud hold out his hand. This is the best part in no way dimmed by Philadelphia wherever it is. He always had it in for . . .

"You wonderful, marvelous beast! You are so beautiful! So deliciously animal! I squirm at the thought!" She take a handful of credits out of shoulder bag. She push them at him and he take, joy all overed.

He turn to go but she stop him with her hand. She very curious tourist. She so curious she don't know electric chair is clinical definition of tourist shock, which is worse being than culture shock as tourist is shocker and object touristed against is shockee. But what did she know?

"Don't you feel bad?" she ask. "Don't you feel bad about killing? Doesn't anything in your beastly state bother you? It's so refreshing!"

He want no chatter. Is time to bounce shoes, to eat before art replace life and he become artistic symmetry of skeletonhood, apprenticeship not so wanted, art being everybody. Also he worry art replace life so quickly, all best restaurants be snapped up fore he get there.

So he just shrug like camel with consumption.

"How can you do it? I don't understand? How do you do it?" She let go of his arm as she see he want to go.

He guess the obvious and say, "With a gun." And he walk away.

He never understand tourist. Like uncranking self-taught virgin. He put money into pants and it makes hot spot which is only way tourist can be understood. Hot spot so hot it steam him up so cold rain of outside not even bother him.

He aim like highway divider for restaurant, to go eat like stupidness. He come by shoe store. He thinking of it all time too. Thinking of it like hunger. He see the robot clerk sitting in same place as before. He go into store and get his old shoes. He wipe new shoes and put back. He put on old shoes and punch switch on robot clerk.

The robot clerk come awake like traffic jam and make proper polite noises. Stonecloud, he look around like complete stranger. He say, "So many shoes. Ten times my fingers and double my toes. I think I will just take them ones," and he point at the pair of shoes he just bring back.

Robot clerk ask if he want to try them on. Stonecloud just wave grandly, detail too small for bothering with.

"Wrap em up," say Stonecloud.

The robot clerk hand package to him and offer change.

"Keep change," Stonecloud say bighearted as he go out door.

Stonecloud go down street, flap, slosh, with new shoes under arm. He feel so good. He going to eat to stupidness. He going to drink to stupidness. He going to dance to stupidness.

Yes, dance; he not be ashamed to dance now. He had paid for his shoes.

PIANO BIRD

In the nightclub there, he smiled at her in the key of G. Maybe he wouldn't have smiled if he had known she was once the smallest thing in the known universe. Maybe. She kept leaning over the end of the piano, staring at him from the bottom of a mixed drink. The slightest breeze would tip her over. She was smashed, trainwrecked, and dizzy on the end that blows bubbles and pops the champagne corks. Her eyebrows were surprised-looking, arched like something Roman, maybe architectural.

Bent over like that, with the top half of her top draped on the edge of the piano and with that kind of dress, the bartender was getting ready to come out from behind the bar and grab her by the shoulder and tell her that they didn't have a license for that kind of thing. It was that kind of thing, too, if she didn't stop vibrating.

No matter how much of her fell out the front of her dress, she was shrinking. Her feet barely touched the floor. So it goes, when you're on the way to becoming the smallest thing in the known universe again.

And in the eyes of those around her, she was small. Getting smaller all the time. Just like Alice. Even birds would now mistake her for something to eat. She was small because she had had days when you could buy her like a souvenir, so tacky and tourist cheap you'd be afraid to take it home. She came out of a long line of souvenirs. Her parents were two holes in the night out of which she tumbled genetically. Her inheritance consisted of unprinted instructions on how to live on air. Genetically blue eyes like industrial diamonds and a high-school scrapbook that hated her so much for being the daughter of nobody, it didn't choose her as the girl most likely.

She leans on the piano, like a featured attraction without a body, only architecture and bust lessons by correspondence. She's got a double smile of lipstick on a full mouth that has always been a little too empty. Her heart is made out of gold because it doesn't have any calories. She stretches herself, leaning way over, trying to touch her lover's ribs, and says, somewhat sarcastically, "You come in like a giant and go out like a dwarf."

That kind of statement could be a curtain raiser, but here she says it casually because she is casual about life in the deadened way that comes naturally to one who has lived. If death was a sexual experience, she'd greet it with a fresh pot of coffee and clean sheets. Nothing more, nothing less.

He pounds the piano nightly. He is like a prayer kneeling in the snow, combing musical notes out of a blank space in his life. He knows one thing. When you sing, your mouth speaks and your mind doesn't have to. He tries to ignore her, singing lightly to the bar stools. To the floor.

He sings and his song says, "I found this empty thing and I emptied it." It is like a comment.

She is like a reply. She says without words, "I will smile at you with irrepressible hormones." Several parts of her body are carefully arranged for smiling. Live ammunition is the only thing she knows how to handle. She knows he knows that too.

He is terrified in a dull way. He senses she is about to give out with one big breath to blow out all the candles of his night. He'd met her once before, in the worst way. He swallows the inside of his throat and misses a chord, musical. If he doesn't sense impending disaster, his fingers do. They sense that she will make a scene and, because of it, the fingers will do something they will regret. They will become unemployed and that is what they will regret.

If she speaks again, it is going to be a conversation, and she does and it is. "I know you're old enough to be rubbery but are you old enough to stretch to the required length?" After that jab, she smiles with the last lilac of the evening dangling out of her mouth like a tongue depressor. She bounces her top emphatically on the edge of the piano, posed there like a left-handed glove on a right-handed ball-player. If the words weren't getting through to him, she knew the bounces would.

Something gets through to him. His smile takes on a frozen-fish look and his fingers become more mindlessly mechanical. He is losing control of himself and his audience. This was not part of the program. Drinking wore away the first half of his strength. His ex-wife, who thought highly of herself, considered herself entitled to waste the second half. He did his life's work with the rest. This woman on the edge of the piano with the face of mistreated lover was breaking the rules. First you break a window and then you become one. Nothing else exists. Nothing else can touch you.

There is a soft, sexual twilight of revenge on her face. A deserted oasis beside her in her bed one night had prepared her for this moment. He had left her once, sneaking silently away into the night. The note beside the bed said, "I WAS GLAD TO GET IT FREE BUT THE IDEA OF MARRIAGE IS TOO GROSS TO BE ADEQUATELY CONSIDERED." It took her six months to find him again.

He has stopped singing even though his fingers continue to move across the keyboard. She unloosened one strap of her gown, pushing it down off her shoulder. More of her fell out of the front of her dress. The bartender wiped his hands nervously and began his journey around the edge of the bar. Under his breath, he was using her gown to wipe the beer glasses clean, but duty was duty.

"My life is a box in which I have been packed and out of which I took myself," she said, and she pulled the other strap loose and began undressing.

The gown fell away in a heap at her feet. She wore nothing beneath it.

But.

But her body was covered with feathers. Her breasts ended in two exaggerated plumes. A ruff of feathers covered the front of her lap.

Silence spreads through the nightclub and even the piano falls prey to it. She leaps free of her clothes, a pioneer moment. She spreads her arms in a taking-flight motion and turns to face the shocked patrons of the nightclub. The feathers look like they grew there naturally.

The bartender, halted in mid-stride, points a silent accusation at her and just stands there, overwhelmed with something. The nightclub manager, alarmed by the sudden silence, stuck his head out of his office door. He sniffed suspiciously for the telltale tear-gas odor of police protection. His gaze took in the bartender and the piano player and then came to rest on the piano bird. He snorted with disgust, ducked his head back inside, and slammed the door with a vicious bang. He vowed to fire them both if the police became involved. He didn't have a license for that kind of thing. Only the police had a license for that.

Some of the looks she was getting were pretty hot but it was cold in the nightclub, even with feathers.

"You asked for it!" she screamed. "Go ahead! Pluck me!"

The piano bird. They came and took her away.

The piano bird. She screamed, "Pluck me!"

But a certain militancy about the feathers scared them all away.

When she tells the cop with stomach distress who books her downtown that she is probably not innocent, he ignores her. He is grimly efficient, so bored with routine, the feathers she wears go by him without drawing a comment. She is here because she is a sentimental eagle. As a species, she is on the endangered list. She returns all the letters her mother back in Minneapolis, Minnesota, sends, marked RETURN TO SENDER BECAUSE OF TOO MANY CONTENTS.

The cop applies the ink, gestures, "Now the thumb in this block here."

She lets him place her thumb firmly against the fingerprint ID card. She says, "I never had much carnal knowledge, but I did send a heat wave from the coast." She seems wistful. If dimpled cheeks can be called a performance, she is smiling.

"Press your thumb evenly but firmly in the second block, too," he says, thinking of the Alka-Seltzer in his desk.

"Aren't you going to ask me why I did it?" she asks, noticing that there are no ripcords on the window blinds in the police station. No one ever bails out here.

For that statement, she gets a fisheye from the cop. All the nuts come out at night. He could have been a mailman.

"Now the index finger. Firmly but evenly."

She was giving him this stare, so he shrugged. "Ok, sure. Why did you do it?" He could care less.

"I opened the lid, I peered into the pot of my life, and the menu flew up my nose. I saw all the places where I ate breakfast, lunch, and dinner. My life had been a varicose-veined waitress who worked too hard for her money. Life had shown me, ultimately, only the space between my legs."

"Oh, Jesus!" said the cop. "They always come out on my shift! If that's a reason, then I'm a . . ."

"But it is. Because you taught me to, taught me it was the only thing I could do."

"Huh?" muttered the cop, shaking his head. "Lady, I

didn't teach you nothing! I don't even know ya, fa chris-
sakes!"

"I know you didn't. You never did but I only very recently learned that."

"Now the other hand," said the cop, trying to look anywhere in the room where she wasn't.

"Ask me why I took my clothes off in public," she said.
"Ask me why I got tired of becoming the smallest thing in
the known universe."

"The other hand," repeated the cop.

"I'll tell you why," said the piano bird. "It's because I'm
in love, in love with all the faces in the dark I never knew.
Maybe even with you."

"Jesus!" said the cop, looking around to see if anybody
overheard her.

"But I wore these feathers because I wanted everyone to
know that no one is going to have me again. No one is going
to own me because I am giving myself to the wind."

They put her in a featureless room. They stripped her of
her feathers. They locked the feathers up in a locker with
the clothes she discarded back at the nightclub. They left
her sitting on a bench, naked.

Then a police matron with cold hands came into the room
and frisked her.

TO SEE THE CITY SITTING
ON ITS BUILDINGS

He was one of the last old people of summer and he came out on a hill, maybe the only one left. They were gathered there. The old, the young, and the no longer restless, all gathered. And he sat by the cold fires and, not knowing or caring if any listened, he said, "I will go do what I have to do." The trees and birds listened. The people listened. It was a time when all things listened, for there were soon to be none left to speak.

The people looked at him like birds seeing torn feathers. They said, "The world ends tonight. You cannot leave your song here and go. Do not leave your song here. It will warm itself by the fire. It will wait for you by the fire. But not for long." All this was said with turned-away faces and silence.

They said, "Do not go. Your song will go outside to wait for you when you do not return. It will set away from the fire. It will get cold." This was said with busy motions and precious moments. That is what they said.

"Tomorrow is cold for all songs," he said and they knew he was right. They knew he was right.

"I will go," he said.

"How will you go?" they asked.

"I will go as an owl. I will go see the city sitting on its buildings." And quietly like a hawk coming without claws, he went away over the soft ground.

And the people shook their heads as he went. And the old

ones, thinking of him, could not see his face in their minds. He was an owl and owls, when the world ends, say, "Don't look at me with your eyes."

There was a place he went to first. It was above the city. It was a high place built of concrete and steel on ground where once a hill stood. It was built there so that one could take pictures of the city to send home. He was not there to send pictures home.

He who had lived his life in a long shadow of a city now felt the first moment of going from a darkened room out into the light. Somewhere down there in the shadow of the city, the sky was hidden. He knew his strength by the distance he could see, and down there in the city, he would be blind and bent in shadows. But he had to go down there. And the world was ending and all of the city was ending. In his heart he knew it was ending, knew that the gray place that did not live was ending but his heart knew it was not enough.

He drew his arm across his face in a wing-and-feather motion, shielding his eyes from the sharp face of the sun. Softly like a bird he moved, like a bird about to soar. He said, "I will fascinate you. I will tear out your eyes with spirit teeth."

And he laughed and laughed.

And below him, the city sat on its buildings.

And he laughed and laughed.

And Detroit screamed on its wheels.

And Chicago slid on slaughtered animals.

And the old man sucked it up in his breath. The panic of an animal city was like telltale smoke to an owl.

And Los Angeles waited like a pregnancy in unmoving traffic.

And the skyline of New York, for the first time, did not cast any shadows.

And the old man tore it away like cobwebs and laughed and laughed.

And the closed eyes of animals, with their heads to the ground, moved slowly with flies.

And the old man saw it. He saw the city burning. The concrete, the steel, the brick and iron, all burning. And the wood of dead trees was rusting. And he laughed, sharpening claws he never had. And there was a song, a little song from his memory and it too was burning.

And the song said, "Go to sleep and do not cry. Your mother is dead and still you feed upon her breasts." That is what the song said. It was the end-of-the-world song of a hungry spider who spins his last web, knowing how to die.

Back there on the hill, the old man's song got cold waiting for him. And the people set all the dances on fire. All the dances on fire. And they packed them away still burning, with handfuls of dirt, red earth like pipestone. They gave the dances all burning to mother earth. Only mother earth can keep dances when the world ends.

The old man stood in the harsh glare of the city, wrapped in the soft protection of folded wings of memory. The air around him was alive with flame as his memories got stronger and the earth moved beneath him with the power of living before him and after him. He felt the earth moving under his feet like a child spinning around and around in a secret place known only to boys. Tomorrow was cold and burnt away to ash. But in the secret place that lived yet inside of him, the current was slow and the warm brown river seemed to be standing still.

And the reason that had sent him away from the hill, when the people gathered, came up the brown river and he could not say her name. No, he could not say her name. Not even now when the world ends could he say her name. For the dead take their names with them out of the world.

But he thought of her in this time of the coming back, in this time of the world ending and coming out of the ground. His old woman had not come out of the ground. That was

why he was there. That was why he was there to see the city
sitting on its buildings.

There to see the city that had hidden the sky. The other
people had buried their city on her grave.

He listened. He did not hear the scratching of her fingers
as she clawed at the city above her. Or did he? Was the long
animal cry of the city her cry, too? Was it her moving-in-
the-grave sound?

The ears of an owl are sharp and he listened. And then he
knew he heard her. The owl can hear many things when the
world ends, and he heard her. The scratching, the painful
scratching of her moving.

"She cannot come up through the sidewalk concrete," he
said. That is what he said. And in his face he took her hammer and beat her name into ashes and beat those ashes into
a hammer. But the spirit calling of her to come was not
enough. They had buried a city on her grave.

He closed his eyes and he said, "I will wait and watch. I
will not go down there yet. I will not speak and see if they
do not move the city. They do not need the city anymore.
Maybe they will tear it down now."

He was an owl and that is what he said.

But they did not move the city. He waited and watched.
An owl waited and watched but they did not move the city.
The other people had buried their city. It was behind them
even though they still lived in it. They had buried their city.

He was an owl and he knew this. He had heard them. He
saw them through the eyes of sick animals. The sun was
going to come at them and they had gathered together like
a swarm of locusts. They were like storm-frightened cattle
and the wings of frightened birds brought their words to
him. They said, "Let's swim to the moon."

He was an owl and that is what they said.

The old man looked up at the flaming sky of high-sun
time. It was hot like a pot oven and the sun was spinning

like a wounded spider, dangling closer to its prey on a single strand of fire. It filled the sky and moved quickly to the west. Moving fast like a thrown spear, the sun pulled night after it like a blanket. It was dark coming at noon. It was the end of the world coming and darkness and flames. Flames and then darkness.

"I am an owl. I live in the dark. I will not be angry when it grows dark."

That was what he said but things within him snapped like twigs in the summer and he sat down on the ground like an old man. He sat down like an old man.

"I am not an owl!" he cried and he beat the ground with fists, not wings.

"I shall fascinate you. I shall tear out your eyes with spirit teeth," he said, and he laughed and laughed and the sound of his laughter was a noise in a hollow barrel and the warm tears ran out of his eyes into the ground. He was an old man. And old men cry when the world ends.

Back on the hill they were gathered. His song had grown cold. His song had no relatives. All his relatives were gone. They could not be there. The other people had buried their cities on them and the sun could not see them down there under the city.

And in the city, in buildings called museums, there were rustling sounds and weeping sounds. In cold gray filing cabinets, the bones of the old ones stirred uneasily. In vaults, in labeled boxes, the bones of the old ones cried restlessly and they could not get free. In one box the leg, an arm in another, the skull filling with tears in a long display case in another room. And the sun could not reach them and mother earth could not bring them awake and they wept, quietly, quietly, in the museums. And they wept.

The old ones, and the young ones, and the no longer restless ones were sitting quietly on the hill. They talked and laughed with their relatives. Far away on something like a hill, the owl knew what they said. They said, "It is a good day today." They said, "We have today and each other. It is a good day to die." And behind all these words, they said one other thing and that was a shy thing that could not be spoken. So it was said with a time of quiet, or a soft look, or a touch. It was said between father and child, between man and woman, with quiet movements that brought them together. All together. They were there with the ground people and the animal people. All together. They were there and the world was ending and they were there. And with faces, not words, they said, "No one here gets out alive."

There was a cold thing coming out of the old man's heart. His cold song had come for him. The wind had blown his song away and it had come for him.

The people on the hill did not see his song blow away, because in the last of the time left they only had eyes for each other, only had eyes for those of their own kind, and he had told them he was an owl. That is what he told them. They could not see his face, all silver and golden, in their minds. They thought he was an owl and owls, when the world ends, say, "Don't look at me with your eyes."

Buried animal and ground people were trying to reach out through the cracks in sidewalks. The ground people moved restlessly under the concrete.

"I will fascinate. I will roll my dead fist in your dead eyes." He raised his fist at the city and did not laugh. He could hear her under the concrete, scratching, scratching.

The world was ending but the city did not know. There were corpses in clown suits running across each other's bodies on rat legs in the city. There were awkward throats moving out of habit, saying, "Pile the bodies here and here and here."

Cheated monkeys with jaded tongues screamed across the

years, saying, "I promised to drown myself." Loud noises choked small throats and softly, softly, like whining children who write on walls, they tumbled over each other in the darkness of a city that sat on its buildings. And the city did not see an old man take a hammer from a store with a broken window. And the city did not see an old man with a hammer trying to move a city.

He swung and hit and swung and hit but cities are dead and forever when the world ends. He broke the hammer. The hammer broke on the concrete. And broken, he sat down like an old man and said, "I want my old woman," and his voice was a tearing sound. "I am not an owl. I want my old woman." This is what he said and his fists hid his eyes and his shoulders shook.

There was a man with a book down there in the city. He was all blood and death and writing in a page and he touched the old man on the shoulder with his book. He touched the old man on the shoulder and he spoke. His ancient words went through the air like a knife and his book was bound in snakeskin. But the old man had been an owl. The bookman ran away. He ran away holding his book with his knees.

It was getting hot like a summer-grass fire and the old man looked up. But the sky was hidden by the city. He had come to the city to find his old woman and now he had lost the sky in the city that hid it. And old men and owls need the sky when the world ends.

He wanted to run away from there. He wanted to fall asleep watching the sky but he could not leave his old woman. He could not run. His song was gone in the wind now and he could not go.

He had gone to see the city sitting on its buildings and now the sky he could not see began to burn him. And the darkness was crawling across his shoulders. And the moon above was there in the hidden sky, chased by dead wishes. The moon was there. The blood moon was there, burning.

Hurting old men, hiding its mother, the city sat on its buildings when the world ended.

And the sky came apart like a wing tearing off.

A HORSE OF A
DIFFERENT TECHNICOLOR

I can remember when the years changed; I can remember when I rode a horse of a different technicolor. Now when I feel like having a woman, I have myself changed into one. You remember me. I was Mr. and Mrs., I rode across your screen. I danced for you. I fell off horses for you. I got shot for you. I was living in two worlds and Jesus Christ was working the night shift. When they said do a rain dance, I did a rain dance. When the dance called for a woman, I was one. You remember me, don't you? If you do, tell me who I am. Am I the book? The movie? I can remember when I rode a horse of a different technicolor. I'm making sense to you, yes I am, unless I am a movie and you are a book.

The universe is divided into two worlds. Now the appeal of two worlds is the fear of death. One world is the book and there it is written, "All lives are to be divided into two sections, day and night." The other world is the microphone and the camera and there it is recorded for playback, shining to us, "I am the kingdom and the glory. Let the children come unto me for they shall be recreated in my own image."

It all began in 2074, twice, once for day and once for night. This story began in 2074 where precedence became the word as it was spoken. THE WORD. Man learned that all men had to rechannel their aggressions. They invented spectators. They said people should be great and disinterested souls. We know the past. We must act accordingly. Yes, let us act accordingly.

The year of 2074 was the year of the success, the all inclusion, the triumph of the wait and watch. They learned how to make people act accordingly. (Do you remember when you wondered whether the people you watched on television could watch you? Now you know, don't you?) And 2074 happened twice. Once in the soil and once in the spirit and they all began acting accordingly. Next year will be the third year 2074 happened; 2074 will always be with us. That is what they said. Did you listen?

I listened and did not learn. I couldn't be the language. I couldn't hide in the same time, couldn't stand for the old, or whisper soft things counting me to sleep like tallied sheep. They pushed my button. I know they pushed my button. I heard the connections made in my brain. I died in my sleep and was changed into someone else on a silver screen. I used to be a book. I'm a lie. I know I'm a lie but I am very important. That makes all the difference. You can be punished for not listening.

(COCKTAIL CONVERSATION TAPE, HOME OF IRON EYES CODY, HOLLYWOOD, CALIFORNIA, 2074— Please file under possible blackmail material.)

Did we push your brain button? Did you die in your sleep? Will you ever know if we made you into someone else? If we changed you from a movie to a book? Did your whole life flash before your eyes at the last moment? Remember, we saved you from 2075. And only white men flash through their lives at the last moment, only white men want to watch home movies. Remember, we saved you from 2075. Trust us. Be true to yourself, ethnic one, less you be undone, as it is, in playback. The signal fades with every playback. Save your strength. Magnetism loves you, be kind to its home, the tape. Remember, you have your place with your race and are taped accordingly. Take your hand off the silver screen. We don't want to push your brain button. You are the book, and as we told you many times before, you can't re-edit anymore. Put your faith in the tape, rest your mind, we shall watch you watch us, we shall not unwind. Spectators are participators. Do not make us push your brain button. Repeat. Do not make us push your brain button.

Finish that moccasin, make it accordingly. Sew that bead choker today. Do it for the tape, for your records must be complete. Nobody likes to push your brain button. Stay tuned.

(THIS INFORMATION BROADCAST ON A CELLULAR LEVEL AS A PUBLIC SERVICE TO ETHNIC MINORITIES, CHANNEL, CODE, AND REVISIONS AS SPECIFIED. THIS BIOCAST SPONSORED BY THE CHURCH OF LATTER DAY ELECTRONIC ENGINEERS. REMEMBER, WE'LL SEE YOU AT THE BOX OFFICE NEXT SUNDAY. AND MAY ALL YOUR HOLOGRAMS, BE HAPPY ONES.)

We made you whole. We made you fit the pattern. We broadcast day and night. We make decisions for you. Take your hand off the silver screen. You are interfering with the projectionist. Yes, we listen, we tell you, you are a book, and having been written, you cannot cancel a line of it. Act accordingly.

(ALL TRANSFORMATIONS ARE CLEAR. FORGIVE US OUR TRANSMISSIONS, DONE WHILE YOU SLEEP, AS YOU LAY IN YOUR BED, A HAND OF HOPE CRUMPLED UNDER YOUR CHEEK.)

Remember when we wondered how technology would affect us? Then we woke up suddenly, not enjoying the long, long journey and at that moment a jet screamed through the air, whipping across the sky like a death overhead. On the beach, children tried to leap into a jet's shadow. How fleeting we were.

(FROM THE SUPPRESSED VIDEOPOEMS OF IRON
EYES CODY.)

I used to be a dancer now I'm happily possessed. I used to sinfully clothe myself in the central facts of our time. Now, because of the lucky cleavage of men into actors and spectators, I remain undressed.

I know you care; I know you'll never cut across my transmission lines. I'll learn and look. I'll promise to remember to forget. I pledge allegiance to the logo and to the station for which it stands.

Forgive me, sponsor, forgive me talking toothbrush for missing a tooth yesterday morning. I am going to make you proud of me. You'll see a change in my overnight ratings, I promise. No longer will the back of my antenna be resistant to your signal. I am going to be better. I will be content with the "given" in sensation's quest. Before your very eyes, in one stunning montage, in one brilliant, symbolic lap dissolve, you'll see me faithful to the screen, see me metamorphosed from an untamed body dancing on trees to a pair of eyes staring beautifully in the dark.

(A CHILD'S PRAYER OF CONTRITION, BAPTIST
HYMNAL, 2074.)

"Remember the Alamo! Send free laxatives to Mexico!"

(IRON EYES CODY IN A SPEECH TO DAVY
CROCKETT—edited out of late-late-show telecast.)

I know they pushed my button. I used to be the best Iron Eyes Cody that was ever Iron Eyes Cody. Yes, I really think I was. I was always built for action. I fell off horses so well. I got shot very beautifully. I was always very graceful. I was always built for action but I never got the girl. No, I never got the girl. I used to wonder why I never got the girl. Then they rewrote the script and I got the girl by getting myself. I always fell off horses so beautifully.

(NOTE FOUND IN MURINE BOTTLE, HOLLY-
WOOD, CALIFORNIA, 2074.)
I watched while you slept. Wouldn't you be more comfortable sleeping on the other side? We want you happy, we
want you rested. We hope you'll stay tuned, we want you
100 percent refreshed. I'm your mattress monitor and, as
you have guessed, it's time to turn over. Yes, turn over. We
want you to pass the freshness test. We'll treat you like a
guest. Roll over; you are done on that side. For your resting
convenience, we are very soft and very wide.

Roll over now; we'll show you how. Do it now; don't
delay. We want you at your best. You are our favorite guest.
We are the ones to count on to prepare you for a perfect
day. Turn over; don't delay. We talk to your kidneys; we are
in constant touch. We hope you'll obey. We don't ask much.
Failure to comply, we make the kidneys let go. Repeat. Failure to comply, we make the kidneys let go. Isn't it better
when the bed stays dry?

(NEURAL TRANSMISSION BROADCAST SPON-
SORED BY THE EXERCISE WHILE YOU SLEEP CITI-
ZENS ACTION COALITION, A LEISURE SERVICE OF
THE NETWORK PRESIDENT'S ADVISORY COMMIS-
SION ON NOCTURNAL EMISSIONS.)
We don't like the way the toilet flushes. It seems un-
diplomatic. We wonder. Could its sound be put in harmony?
Can you change the rhythm, mute the gurgle, accentuate
the flush? We only tell you this because you are near and
dear to us. We want your home sounding just right. We
want you happy, day and night. We don't want to mention
it. We really hate to mention it. We hate to mention it but
we count. We measure. We are here to insure your utmost
in living pleasure. We recommend prunes. We want to see
more of you here. You know the danger of becoming a
stranger. Wipe away your gloom; let us help you here in the
bathroom. We tell you one thing our findings show—you

could come here more times than you wanted to go. Trust us
and change that flush.

(TOILET DISPENSER BROADCAST, WORDS AND
LYRICS BY AMERICA'S FOREMOST VIDEOPOET—
JAMES DEAN. Remember we touch you deeply.)

As you approach sign-off, take comfort in the path of
transmission. Remember as you travel through life, the
world has got you by the golden apples. Take comfort for
your future is now, now and forever more now. It is audio-
visual. Stay tuned. For happiness the number to call is—. Ask
for George or Candy. Or both. We are glad you have chosen
our lens as the one to look at. We are glad to see you. Be assured we see you. No one ever dies. Repeat. Take comfort
that no one ever dies. Although the original telecast has
ceased, we promise you shall live on in reruns and syndica-
tion. Take comfort in your longevity. Take comfort, we say.
Channel Ten has picked up your option. Your life will be
continued as a children's program. The "Uncle Burping
Buffalo Show." We have signed F. Scott Fitzgerald to play
the buffalo. Rejoice in transmission everlasting.

(OFFICIAL FUNERAL TELECAST OF FIRST
DRUNKEN WOODEN INDIAN. THIS STATION IS
PROUD TO CARRY THE INDIAN FATHER OF HIS
COUNTRY. "PERHAPS YOU HAVE SEEN HIS FACE ON
THE NICKEL. HE'S THE ONE WITHOUT THE
HUMP," SAID THE HIRED FUNERAL COMEDIAN.)

Yes, we wrote you as a book, saved you from 2075. Could
you live without what we give? We tell you the truth. Don't
make us push your brain button. You believe in one-armed
men. We made you whole and we don't like that very much.
We feel, your voice and image is wavering from our purpose. It is becoming soft, muted. We want more lights on
your face. Remember, we saved you as a representative of
your race. We monitor, we pray, and we teach. Are you trying to escape our reach? Why do you dream of 2075? We

checked, we programmed, we wrote the book. Be glad you're alive. Be glad you have 2074 just once more. You are the kingdom and the book. Watch me dance on the silver screen. There are no words to confuse you. There are no painful choices. No fear of right or wrong. There are no choices to confuse you. We offer you the appeal of two words, fear and death. The fear of death. Do you know what we mean? WON'T YOU WATCH US DANCE ON THE SILVER SCREEN?

(TAPED LIVE AT THE HOUSE OF PERFORMANCE IN CALIFORNIA, COPYRIGHT REASONABLE PERSUASION MUSIC CO., ALL RIGHTS RESERVED, 2074. Music to be reasonably persuaded by.)

Remember we made and remade every dream ever played and put them on the screen. We wrote the book. We asked nothing of you, wanted nothing of you, programmed nothing from you. We came into your home. Did you look? Don't make me ask you again. We don't want to push that button. We don't want to send you to that place where lights close their tired eyes. Remember one-armed men carry imaginary fists at the end of imaginary arms.

(THE PRECEDING MESSAGE FED INTRAVENOUSLY TO GERIATRIC PATIENTS, CHANNEL, CODE, AND REVISIONS AS SPECIFIED. REMEMBER THE MOTTO OF SENIOR CITIZENS PARIMUTUEL BETTING INC.—ONLY FOOLS BET AGAINST THE POOLS. DON'T DIE WITHOUT PLACING A BET—YOUR TIME COULD BE OUR TIME—AND YOU MIGHT WIN YET.)

This is strictly confidential, but I thought you'd like to know I've been watching you and your hormone count is really quite low. I hope you can correct this. I've watched you; I've programmed your text. Biologically speaking, this monitor recommends sex. Please act accordingly. Your audience loves you. Love them. Refill the lifely cup; we want to see your hormone production go up.

(THIS BROADCAST IMPLANTED WITH YOUR NEVER-SLEEPS INTRA-UTERINE DEVICE. THIS TAPE WILL SELF-CORRUPT IN THIRTY SECONDS.) Was your voice unsynchronized with the image? Was the meaning hidden, the lights too bright? It came out wrong. It was not what we hoped. Believe me, it will not happen again. Buttons will be pushed, brains will roll. Yes, we know we made an error; we have discovered error. Did we miscalculate your sex? Watch the screen. Watch the screen. See us rectify the errors. Remember editors make mistakes. We wrote the book. We edited the movie for you. Be patient. If you've discovered a mistake in the year 2074, consider it was put there on purpose. We try to put something in 2074 for everybody and some people are always looking for mistakes.

(THIS TAPE BROADCAST ON THE EACH FIRST DAY OF THE SECOND COMING TIME OF THE GRAND AND GLORIOUS YEAR 2074. THIS IS THE SEVENTY-SECOND BROADCAST OF THIS JOYFUL MESSAGE, BROUGHT TO YOU ONCE EACH 2074, courtesy of the unemployed calendar-printers' union.)

I HAVE SEEN THE FUTURE AND I WON'T GO.
(popular folksong from 2074.)
(Crazy Horse, his dying words, 1876.)

I can't help you anymore, tell the people I cannot help anymore. (AS THE DIRECTOR, I HAVE DECIDED THAT THE ROLE OF CRAZY HORSE MUST BE REWRITTEN. IN THE MOVIE VERSION, WE WILL HAVE HIM SAY "ONLY BY MY DEATH CAN I HELP MY PEOPLE; ONE SMALL STEP FOR MAN; ONE GIANT LEAP AT THE BOX OFFICE." IN PLACE OF HAVING HIM MURDERED BY CAVALRY OFFICERS WHO STABBED HIM IN THE BACK, WE ADD A CHASE SCENE WHERE HE ESCAPES FROM PRISON,

RAPES AND MURDERS A TWELVE-YEAR-OLD GIRL, AND IS FINALLY DRIVEN TO COMMIT SUICIDE OUT OF GUILT. THE PRODUCER AGREED TO IT ONLY ON THE CONDITION THAT JOHN WAYNE PLAY THE TWELVE-YEAR-OLD GIRL.)

I knew you'd see it my way. I knew careful editing would make the meaning clear. It was wrong of you to want 2075. It was wrong of you to assume that our art needed you, the spectator, in order to be. It was wrong. The film can run, the tape can play without you. YOU CANNOT EXIST WITH-OUT IT. We insure your existence. We married you when none would have you. We had you. We had you. We had you.

When we start a film, we put out the lights.

(From the Webster's dictionary, printed 2074, SUICIDE —1: an unprogrammed act, usually committed without bene-fit of monitoring devices. Usually a fatal act, a fatal taking of one's life, without being ordered to do so, or recording the act for rebroadcast. 2: A sin of nontransmission at a mo-ment of the highest entertainment value.)

This is an official notification to all those suicide-prone people who insist on depriving their peers from witnessing their death. In order to insure that the people are not de-prived of the entertainment due them, we have devised a method of taking still pictures of your body and turning it into a film for broadcast purposes. We take the still picture of your dead body, assemble the dead pictures on a travel-ing matte, and, through recent innovations of the multiplane camera, bring it to life as a film by artificial insemination. This is the meaning and aim for our films. This is an official notification to suicide-prone monitor tamperers. The people must not be denied their entertainment. Please confine your deaths to monitored periods. The people must not be denied entertainment. Civilization must not aspire for 2075. It is not on the program. Read this book. It is a suicide note. The people must not be denied their entertainment.

(Please watch your monitor. I am committing suicide. The people must not be denied their entertainment. Stay tuned. The people must not be—)

You are now watching a test pattern. The pleasing tone is designed for your listening enjoyment. Our test pattern is designed to be symmetrically pleasing. Are you happy?

The truth about the evils of happiness is on Channel Thirteen. Please change your dial for this channel. Repeat. Please change your dial for the truth about the evils of happiness.

TIME DEER

The old man watched the boy. The boy watched the deer. The deer was watched by all and the Great Being above.

The old man remembered when he was a young boy and his father showed him a motorcycle thing on a parking lot.

The young boy remembered his second life with some regret, not looking forward to the coming of his first wife.

Tuesday morning the Monday morning traffic jam was three days old. The old man sat on the hood of a stalled car and watched the boy. The boy watched the deer. The deer was watched by all and the Great Being above.

The young boy resisted when his son, at the insistence of his bitch of a white wife, had tried to put him in a rest home for the elderly. Now he watched a deer beside the highway, and was watched in turn.

The old man was on the way to somewhere. He was going someplace, someplace important; he forgot just where. But he knew he was going.

The deer had relatives waiting for her, grass waiting for her, season being patient on her account. As much as she wanted to please the boy by letting him look at her, she had to go. She apologized with a shake of her head.

The old man watched the deer going. He knew she had someplace to go, someplace important. He did not know where she was going, but she knew why.

The old man was going to be late. He could have walked. He was only going across the road. He was going across the road to get to the other side. He was going to be late for his

own funeral. The old man was going someplace. He couldn't
remember where.

"Did you make him wear the watch? If he's wearing the
watch, he should—"

"He's an old man, honey! His mind wanders," said Frank
Strong Bull.

"Dr. Amber is waiting! Does he think we can afford to
pay for every appointment he misses?" snarled Sheila, running her fingers through the tangled ends of her hair.
"Doesn't he ever get anywhere on time?"

"He lives by Indian time. Being late is just something you
must expect from—" he began, trying to explain.

She cut him off. "Indian this and Indian that! I'm so sick
of your goddamn excuses I could vomit!"

"But—"

"Let's just forget it. We don't have time to argue about it.
We have to be at the doctor's office in twenty minutes. If we
leave now, we can just beat the rush-hour traffic. I just hope
your father's there when we arrive."

"Don't worry. He'll be there," said Frank, looking doubtful.

But the deer could not leave. She went a little distance
and then turned and came back. And the old man was
moved because he knew the deer had come back because
the boy knew how to look at the deer.

And the boy was happy because the deer chose to favor
him. And he saw the deer for what she was. Great and
golden and quick in her beauty.

And the deer knew that the boy thought her beautiful.
For it was the purpose of the deer in this world on that
morning to be beautiful for a young boy to look at.

And the old man who was going someplace was grateful
to the deer and almost envious of the boy. But he was one
with the boy who was one with the deer and they were all

one with the Great Being above. So there was no envy, just
the great longing of age for youth.

"That son of a bitch!" growled Frank Strong Bull. "The
bastard cut me off." He yanked the gearshift out of fourth
and slammed it into third. The tach needle shot into the red
and the Mustang backed off, just missing the foreign car
that had swerved in front of it.

"Oh Christ— We'll be late," muttered Sheila, turning in
the car seat to look out the back window. "Get into the ex-
press lane."

"Are you kidding? With this traffic?"

His hands gripped the wheel like a weapon. He lifted his
right hand and slammed the gearshift. Gears ground, caught
hold, and the Mustang shot ahead. Yanking the wheel to the
left, he cut in front of a truck, which hit its brakes, missing
the Mustang by inches. He buried the gas pedal and the car
responded. He pulled up level with the sports car that had
cut him off. He honked and made an obscene gesture as he
passed. Sheila squealed with delight.

"Go! Go!" she exclaimed.

The old man had taken liberties in his life. He'd had
things to remember and things he wanted to forget. Twice
he had married.

The first time. He hated the first time. He'd been blinded
by her looks and his hands had got the better of him. He
had not known his own heart and, not knowing, he had let
his body decide. It was something he would always regret.

That summer he was an eagle. Free. Mating in the air.
Never touching down. Never looking back. That summer.
His hands that touched her were wings. And he flew and the
feathers covered the scars that grew where their bodies had
touched.

He was of the air and she was of the earth. She muddied

his dreams. She had woman's body but lacked woman's spirit. A star is a stone to the blind. She saw him through crippled eyes. She possessed. He shared. There was no life between them. He saw the stars and counted them one by one into her hand, that gift that all lovers share. She saw stones. And she turned away.

He was free because he needed. She was a prisoner because she wanted. One day she was gone. And he folded his wings and the earth came rushing at him and he was an old man with a small son. And he lived in a cage and was three years dead. And his son was a small hope that melted. He was his mother's son. He could see that in his son's eyes. It was something the old man would always regret.

But the deer, the young boy, these were things he would never regret.

Dr. Amber was hostile. "Damn it! Now look—I can't sign the commitment papers if I've never seen him."

Sheila tried to smile pleasantly. "He'll show up. His hotel room is just across the street. Frank will find him. Don't worry."

"I have other patients! I can't be held up by some doddering old man," snapped Dr. Amber.

"Just a few more minutes," Sheila pleaded.

"You'll have to pay for two visits. I can't run this place for free. Every minute I'm not working, I'm losing money."

"We'll pay," said Sheila grimly. "We'll pay."

The world was big and the deer had to take her beauty through the world. She had been beautiful in one place for one boy on one morning of this world. It was time to be someplace else. The deer turned and fled into the woods, pushing her beauty before her into the world.

The young boy jumped to his feet. His heart racing, his feet pounding, he ran after her with the abandon of youth that is caring. He chased beauty through the world and disappeared from the old man's sight in the depths of the forest.

And the old man began dreaming that—

Frank Strong Bull's hand closed on his shoulder and his son shook him, none too gently.

The old man looked into the face of his son and did not like what he saw. He allowed himself to be led to the doctor's office.

"Finally," said Sheila. "Where the hell was he?"

Dr. Amber came into the room with a phony smile. "Ah! The elusive one appears! And how are we today?"

"We are fine," said the old man, bitterly. He pushed the outstretched stethoscope away from his chest.

"Feisty, isn't he?" observed Dr. Amber.

"Let's just get this over with," said Sheila. "It's been drawn out long enough as it is."

"Not sick," said the old man. "You leave me alone." He made two fists and backed away from the doctor.

"How old is he?" asked Dr. Amber, looking at the old man's wrinkled face and white hair.

"Past eighty, at least," said his son. "The records aren't available and he can't remember himself."

"Over eighty, you say. Well, that's reason enough then," said Dr. Amber. "Let me give him a cursory examination, just a formality, and then I'll sign the papers."

The old man unclenched his fists. He looked at his son. His eyes burned. He felt neither betrayed nor wronged. He felt only sorrow. He allowed one tear, only one tear, to fall. It was for his son who could not meet his eyes.

And for the first time since his son had married her, his eyes fell upon his son's wife's eyes. She seemed to shrivel under his gaze, but she met his gaze and he read the dark things in her eyes.

They were insignificant, not truly a part of his life. He had seen the things of importance. He had watched the boy. The boy had watched the deer. And the deer had been watched by all and the Great Being above.

The old man backed away from them until his back was against a wall. He put his hand to his chest and smiled. He was dead before his body hit the floor.

"A massive coronary," said Dr. Amber to the ambulance attendant. "I just signed the death certificate."

"They the relatives?" asked the attendant, jerking a thumb at the couple sitting silently in chairs by the wall.

Dr. Amber nodded.

The attendant approached them.

"It's better this way," said Sheila. "An old man like that, no reason to live, no—"

"Where you want I should take the body?" asked the attendant.

"Vale's Funeral Home," said Sheila.

Frank Strong Bull stared straight ahead. He heard nothing. His eyes were empty of things, light and dark.

"Where is it?" asked the attendant.

"Where is what?" asked Dr. Amber.

"The body? Where's the body?"

"It's in the next room. On the table," said Dr. Amber, coming around his desk. He took the attendant's arm and led him away from the couple.

"I'll help you put it on the stretcher."

The old man who watched the deer. He had dreamed his second wife in his dreams. He had dreamed that. But she had been real. She had come when emptiness and bitterness had possessed him. When the feathers of his youth had been torn from his wings. She filled him again with bright pieces of dreams. And for him, in that second half of his life, far from his son and that first one, he began again. Flying. Noticing the world. His eyes saw the green things, his lips tasted the sweet things and his old age was warm.

It was all bright and fast and moving, that second life of his and they were childless and godless and were themselves children and gods instead. And they grew old in their bodies, but death seemed more like an old friend than an interruption. It was sleep. One night the fever took her. Peacefully. Took her while she slept and he neither wept nor followed. For she had made him young again and the young do not understand death.

"I'll help you put it on the stretcher."
They opened the door.

And the old man watched the boy and did not understand death. And the young boy watched the deer and understood beauty. And the deer was watched by all and the Great Being above. And the boy saw the deer for what she was. And like her, he became great and golden and quick. And the old man began dreaming that—

Frank Strong Bull's hand, his son's hand, closed on his shoulder and shook him, none too gently.

They opened the door. The body was gone.

The last time it was seen, the body was chasing a deer that pushed its beauty through the world, disappearing from an old man's sight into the depths of the forest.

WHERE THEY PUT
THE STAPLES
AND WHY SHE LAUGHED

Peter Renoir makes an entrance into her apartment. He is impelled by a desire to rebuild a dream in which he can lose himself. It is a conviction indisputably expressed in his choice of a tie. His tie is as broad as the Mississippi delta. It glows in the dark. It is invisible.

Semina was spread-eagled on a quilt in the center of the living room. She has just returned from a canceled engagement at a beauty parlor and is suffering the consequent withdrawal symptoms.

She opens her eyes as he enters and says, "You can achieve enlightenment only by following through to the end an obsession that has its source in a spiritual sickness."

The scene shifts subtly and we can see that Peter Renoir is now spread-eagled on the quilt and it is Semina who is making her entrance into the living room.

She circles the centerfolded man cautiously. She thinks she knows the truth and thus has more of an opportunity to face that amount of it, traditionally denied her. Self-awareness has occurred to her. With startling abruptness, she has become a factor in Peter Renoir's world. Peter Renoir is stunned and experiences a flashback.

He is deeply in love with a girl named Norma Jean, but while still in love with her, he realizes that he himself is

Norma Jean or rather that Norma Jean is potentially within him. He is fourteen years old and his voice is changing.

An old man in a park terrifies him. The old man represents the pitiful inadequacy of human illumination to combat the all-encompassing metaphysical darkness of the world. The old man sat in the park waiting for little boys who looked exactly like Peter Renoir to come along. The old man had escaped from a circus. The old man broke light bulbs between his teeth and did not laugh as he chewed the broken glass and swallowed it. This was the old man's specialty.

Peter ran through the park, late for his violin lesson and he saw the old man. The old man made him sit down on the bench beside him. The shadow cast by the old man covered the boy's face, at one point almost obliterating him.

The old man talks very pleasantly and entices the boy to tell him about his dreams. As the boy begins to talk, his voice cracks. The old man laughs. And it is then that the old man terrifies the young boy. The old man tells Peter that his voice is not changing. No, it is still the same voice.

"It is your ears which are changing," said the old man. "Your ears are bad and one day they will turn into loudspeakers."

Peter ran from the old man in terror. Somehow the old man had instilled in him another set of dreams that had not as yet suggested themselves to him. Rejection. The fear of rejection. He imagined that Norma Jean had agreed to go to the movies with him but, once there, insisted that she be allowed to sit in the row behind him. Further, he imagined that his ears would trumpet out the message, "You don't even want to touch me!" just as she is giving into the temptation to go to the restroom.

Throughout this flashback, our consciousness is split between these two characters. On the one hand, we have the fear of loudspeakers and, on the other, the temptation to go to the restroom. By means of this duality, a tension mounts that is in itself the essence of the tensions in all human relationships. The film approaches the climax. Peter Renoir is afraid to turn around and look at her for fear of missing the end of the movie. Peter is afraid to turn around because Norma Jean might have yielded to temptation behind his back. Norma Jean is afraid to yield to temptation because she too fears that she will miss the end of the movie.

Suddenly, there is a power failure in Minneapolis and the movie theater is plunged into darkness. Peter Renoir is stunned. Norma Jean is stunned.

The lights are out in the restrooms too.

The flashback ends and we are left with Peter Renoir futilely trying to cope with Norma Jean's darkness. In desperation, Peter begins to insist that he sees her, despite the total darkness, that he loves her which forcefully brings home the idea that the Minneapolis Power and Light Company have only very clumsily attempted to destroy a dream. Unknown to the suffering boy, Norma Jean has crawled out of the theater on her hands and knees. When she reaches the street, she explains the experience to herself.

"Naked was I born into the world, and naked I go on the screen again. My only regret is that I had to resort to crawling on my hands and knees to escape the shock of comprehension. If I have materialized my dreams into factories, it was not done in malice; and just because I am THE WOMAN, there is no need to read any religious significance into it."

After this heartfelt confession, we experience the unpleasant sensation of watching a human personality disintegrate before our eyes and she makes one additional statement. "I hope the restrooms in the Greyhound bus depot are clean."

As she leaves, we hear a voice explaining in textbook fashion, "NOW YOU DO THIS . . . NOW YOU DO THAT . . ."

Poor little Peter Renoir, unaware that Norma Jean has left the theater with cinematic style, gazes with fascination into the darkness that surrounds him. He continues to insist that he sees her. That she is behind him, is real and tangible. That she is his, and only his, Norma Jean.

It is at this point that we discover that Peter Renoir is a sick man who once was a sick boy. We begin to sense the irony of his life. As he talks to her empty seat in the darkened theater, we begin to understand that he is in love not with a woman but with an IDEA. He has little awareness of the possibility that he is rejecting life for an unattainable and false IDEA.

He offers to buy popcorn for the idealized vision of her, having substituted her for the darkness of reality. Her silence puzzles him, but he rationalizes it and dreams of taking her erotically on the carpet between the thirty-fourth and thirty-fifth rows of seats. An usher brushes across his face with a flashlight beam.

The usher is about to urge Peter Renoir to be calm, to be cool, and to get the hell out of there since he is the only one left in the movie theater.

The flashback begins before the usher can speak and the old man who eats light bulbs meets a little boy named Peter Renoir in a park. The boy is running to his violin lesson. He is late and his eyes are blinded by the bright sunlight. The little boy has just been ushered out of a darkened theater by a dark usher. The little boy is mired in the quicksands of illusion and reality.

The old man is kind enough to scare the hell out of him. The old man instills in the young boy the awesome fear that life is not Norma Jean being taken erotically on the carpet between the thirty-fourth and thirty-fifth rows of seats in a darkened movie theater but is instead an old man in a park who breaks light bulbs between his teeth and does not laugh as he chews the broken glass and swallows it. This explanation of life was the old man's specialty too.

The flashback ends and Semina is making Peter Renoir a drink. The logs in the fireplace burn merrily. Outside, the snow piles in drifts around their apartment. It is an idyllic setting with soft music moving into the room from the stereo.

Semina hands Peter his drink. Moisture condenses on the outside of the glass and leaves a ring on Peter Renoir's face. Semina picks up the drink, dabbing at the moisture on the magazine page. She smooths out the picture and holds it closer to the fire. Peter Renoir's face swells and wrinkles as the water dries. Semina downs the drink with a satisfied sigh and closes the magazine with an abrupt snap. She pitches it and the centerfold of Peter Renoir into the fireplace where it begins to burn.

Semina saw the place on your body where they made the fold. She saw the place on your body where they put the staples.

She laughed.

A PLACE TO DIE
ON THE PHOTOGRAPH
OF YOUR SOUL

I'm going to die with my feet in the trees. Eating barbed-wire sandwiches. I'm going to live so that all the people who never had the time to get to know me are unaware that I got to know them. I used to be sure that I could buy a stairway to the stars and that there were words I could say that opened all the doors, like something magical you read out of a forgotten book in the dark of night. But books don't bleed and thoughts are often only misgivings.

Take Cassie. Rotten as a playtoy bird. Woman with no eyes and all handed. Makes me wonder if feelings I get are mine altogether or just boats that float through my mental trees. Am I me or something launched by somebody else? I wonder; new days seem old—this morning strangely seems like one I had had before. Am I new and old or young and aging?

Take Cassie. Litany of smothered light, makes me wonder. In women, I have lived, been kicked out squealing. Terrified, I want to fulfill some sort of destiny, be buried someplace else besides in me. Maybe in you. Maybe in the soil of some other Earth.

Have you seen Earth? I mean, really. The funny, sad little molehill towns with names like New York and Pittsburgh. Rabbit hutches or guppy breeding tanks. Something

deranged and artificial, every minute of it. Not anybody's
idea of a vacation. Certainly not mine.

Take Cassie, we call her a drug, demeaning her. We call
her mother night, apple angry. We pinch her dark trees and
climb her fences. Tie her to the side of dawn; aging, we
flame out our hearts, crashing above the mountain ranges of
breasts. Are my feet armored? Have we rested for nothing,
aspired to less?

I aspire to cut, what? Perhaps simply to cut. To hack, to
spew out mediocrities. Let me die; let no women come my
way. Daylight and dark women. Burn them all. Dark
women. What insane thoughts in them? What kind of animals are they?

Do they nest? How often and how sharp the teeth? I have
heard many men's questions and all the good answers have
been given long ago. But call it compulsion, call it what you
will, no barriers exist until we trip over them. Some people
live so furiously, the barriers run from them. Am I a barrier?
I know I run a lot. But no matter, we ramble on. Looking at
what we see, adding what's missing, and making up the rest.

It's a good life, here on the third planet from the sun. I
know it's a good life because when you're number three,
you're a charm. Well, why not? Why not peace and serenity
and dark women in the tumbledown night? If only there
were no dark men, but no matter. We have them convinced
they shouldn't be and that's almost the same.

Take Cassie, and what do I mean. Take Cassandra, ah,
the word itself, in its full length, a truthteller unbelieved in
her time. What a waste of starlight. The legend persists.
Grind it down in the valley below. Seasons are made to forget. Forget it, let the truth oil the wheels, mesh with good
and bad. Use truth for lubrication but keep it trapped in the
machine, endlessly touched by wheels. Busy. Keep the truth
busy. Change its meaning and diapers every day. Speak to
me in circles. I only understand circles.

Cut the rebels with looking glasses and false senses of power. Mirrors praise beauty and we name planets after you and you lubricate as if Cassandra never lived. We photograph the side of stone faces. We photograph, recapture the planes of a face for a special something else, something more. We photograph and freeze moments, while lurking memories move outside the frame. Oh, spin on darkly, mother night. Hold the candles away from the light. Wishful, sinful, wicked too.

The dark fears of primitives are awash here. Don't photograph me. I can't look like that forever. Don't capture my soul, devil box, the beauty hoax. Souls don't look like that except when forced. Rabbit hutches are filled with too many contents, all looking for a place to die on the photograph of their souls. A place to die on the photograph of your soul.

I wonder if you have seen Earth. Golden wasted acres of blame. Graceful fields of forage and bovine creatures, harnessed to photographs of photogenic souls, plowing the literary worlds with foreplay-sharpened elbows. And the hordes that await glitter, they swarm among you, beneath you, in carpools and typing pools, writing indirect memos to the sun, typing double-spaced copy on Art Deco bedsheets. A place to die on the photograph of your soul.

Sail into the wind, Cassandra. The third planet from the sun is hungry for your votes and every vote is a vote and as planned; there is no storm that can drink any more of you than you of it. Only where you spin too loudly, only where you bulge the equators where others have planned something polar and cold for you, perhaps then they will be frightened of you. When you BECOME where formerly you BELONGED, only then will the third planet from the sun, busy with some little war or other, stop for a minute or two. Perhaps the world will uncircle the sun, hold its breath, consider itself in a new light. Perhaps.

Ancient wisdom exists only if you use it, knock down the

azure sky. Touch people with human hands. Cover the rabbit hutch with stolen thunder. The cattle are fat and mean in this weather. They like the grass prechewed. The fences men erect don't fool anybody and they really don't count sheep to put them asleep. They don't.

They're afraid of sheep and what lurks in innocence, buried deep. I am sheep. I toil not in the fields and eat not of the grass therein. I have beautiful jeweled eyes. I live asleep on the blade of a dagger. I crouch in culture fright on the edges of the cities. I await my liberation with eyes that stalk not beauty but power and world-unfearing strength.

Hard sisters, sleep here among the sheep but in the dark, carry scissors. Free us from the wool of men's eyes. Take us away in your strength, take us with you, leave the cattle a place to die on the photograph of their souls. I lose my legs angrily, they fall off in front of tourists and I won't dance anymore. Lose your legs, too. Cut them off the photograph. The ears of the planet and eyes, cut them, trim them out with strong hearts. The blood runs close to the surface, so cut there.

Not temporary cuts, cut deep. Not superficial cuts, cut deep. Take the tops off the mountains, let the forest grow back there. Cut deep and wide and lovingly. Shoot the rifles tenderly. Life is more than the space between your legs. Life is more than a place to die on the photograph of your soul. Carry scissors—shear, snip away into darkling night.

Wound but wisely. Look to each other for strength, back away from unlived life but not from unleashed power. Take the sky away. Take the sky away in your power. Put people in it, send your thoughts up like tree branches. Soft thoughts, keep them for private torment. Think strong.

Wield all things in battle but your bodies. All things in battle but bodies. Man and woman. Not man with woman. Woman and man and child.

The May queen, seeking an equal, picks one; he wears no

wool, is not blind. Live like trees who lose their leaves. Man
and woman. Woman and man. Child. No other way leads
with strength.

A tree without leaves is a trunk, sexless in winter. A taste
of wasted bone on the lips.

A man without woman.

A woman without man.

Like this, a taste of wasted bone on the lips.

Like this, a place to die on the photograph of your soul.

A child is from the strengths of two wisdoms, conceived.
Misunderstood in the light of the present day, voiceless in
the modern ear, it is yet to be. It will change. Nurse the
thought in your strength. It will change.

Have you seen the Earth? Not he or she but we?

Tomorrow may come any day. Watch for it.

WITH THE PAIN
IT LOVES AND HATES

He had the frost of winter in his hair and the slowness of
cooling ashes in his blood. The men in the village did not
know where he came from. One day he was there, standing
under the drying racks, his eyes like two soaring hawks as he
watched the children at play.

Old Bear Teeth went to him but the old one did not
speak. He turned and walked back up the mountain. He
gave no answers to the questions shouted at his back.

He came back again and again. He spoke to no man. He
watched the children. The old chiefs spoke of him and they
were frightened of this old one who would not speak and
whose purpose was unknown. They wrapped their robes
about them and muttered. And there were some who would
kill the old one. On the day that they decided this thing, the
old one came dressed in a faded robe of our clan.

Old Bear Teeth went to the strange one again. "Who are
you, old one?"

The aged one from the mountains looked into the eyes of
Old Bear Teeth. His voice was thick and uneasy upon his
tongue as if it had slept a long time. "My name? It has been
so long since I have used it. So long since I have spoken to
other beings of blood and skin. I was once called Long
Bear."

"Hai!" Old Bear Teeth stepped back. "Long Bear was
from this village! There was a child of that name. But Long

Bear was taken as a child from this place by a demon! Are
you a demon, old one?"

"I was touched by demons. The demons that touch all
men in their deeds and their sleep. I am no demon. Do not
be afraid of me."

"Who are you who says he is Long Bear? I knew Long
Bear as a boy. We played together. The demons took him.
This I remember."

"I am he. Dimly I remember. You were called Running
Elk. That was yours before your man name."

Old Bear Teeth looked deep into the face of the old one.
His dim eyes probed the lines and seams of his face. "Yes it is
so. You are Long Bear. But were you not taken by demons?"

Old Bear Teeth backed farther away. The fear was tight in
the muscles of his face and the hollow of his stomach.

"You need not fear me. I can hurt no one," said the old
one.

"Are you a demon? Do you breathe? Do you sleep? I am
afraid of you, old one, with the name and aged face of one
who went away with the dark ones of the mountains," said
Old Bear Teeth.

"Why are you here, aged one? What do you seek?"

The old one sighed and shook his head. A sad smile appeared and it was full of black meaning. It was the smile of
lizards watching with hidden eyes in the rocks below the
graves of the dead. Old Bear Teeth pulled his robe tight
about his shoulders and hurried away. And the old one came
and went.

With the patience of a snake, the old one came and went,
watching the children. Watching them all, day after day.

The village was full of talk about this strange one who
came and went. The mothers of the village feared for their
children. But none knew why until the day of the death of
the crippled bird.

Little Birch, daughter of Elk Son had gone far, gathering

the berries. In her eagerness to fill her pot, she left the women and other small ones her age.

As she scurried over the ridge, picking berries as fast as her good, bright hands would allow, she heard a little cry.

Crawling over a rock, she found the crippled bird. It was a young hawk with a broken wing. She cried out, seeing it suffer. It was a white-head hawk, lying on its side, crying at the sky.

She set her berry pot down and gathered the crippled bird up in her hands carefully. The bird did not fight her. She walked back down the ridge, the bird held gently in both of her hands.

As she came upon the women, they made noises and gathered to look at the crippled bird. The hawk, angry with the noisy women, hissed and spat at them, trying to peck the ones that touched him. Little Birch pushed them away, shielding the bird with her body. The bird was well settled within her touch.

"Bring the crippled bird to me!"

Little Birch turned in surprise, hearing the harsh words.

Domea, the shaman, beckoned to her. "Come. I want to see this hawk." His tone of speaking was harsh but he was kind behind his eyes.

Little Birch walked through the women and set the bird gently down at Domea's feet. "I found him in the rocks," she said.

The shaman bent over and examined the crippled bird. He spoke softly, trying to touch the bird as Little Birch had touched him. But the hawk shrilled fiercely and scuttled back to Little Birch, dragging his broken wing on the ground.

"You have not found him, he has found you. It is an omen of good. See how he comes to you," said Domea. "The white-head hawk will watch over you and protect you as long as he lives. It is a very good sign."

At his words, Little Birch felt brightness and warm sun flow through her. There were not many good omens for Little Birch and her family. Her father had been struck with the withered arm, and many times, there was little meat because of it. But with the coming of the crippled bird, this changed.

Many deer fell beneath Elk Son's clumsy bow. There was magic in this, the people of the village said. The deer did not run from him, said the old men of the village. It is all because of the white-head hawk that Little Birch cares for with her skill and her love. And for the first time, Little Birch's family had a time of plenty. Now they had meat where others had none.

And they shared their good fortune with others. And of all the children, Little Birch was the most honored among the small ones. Even small ones many snows older than her gave her first choose in the games. And thus things went until the day the crippled bird was killed.

Not all of the small ones honored Little Birch. Blue Snow, the son of Antelope Runs, had only envy and hatred for Little Birch and the crippled bird.

One day while the others were at play in the hills below the village, Blue Snow snuck into Elk Son's lodge and stole the white-head hawk. He put the bird in a basket and ran away into the hills, far from the others.

He took the bird out of its cage. Its wing was almost mended.

"I hate you bird!" he cried and he broke the mending wing. And the bird cried.

"I hate you!" and he threw the bird upon the ground and killed it with big stones. Then he ground his foot on the bird and spat upon it. He hated.

He felt a hand upon his shoulder. He looked up, scared to

be found out. The old one who watched the children looked at him.

"Let me go," said Blue Snow fearfully.

"You enjoyed killing the crippled bird. This is true," said the old one.

Blue Snow looked into the old one's eyes and could not lie.

"Yes! I liked killing it! I hate it! I hate it!"

"You knew what the white-head hawk meant to Little Birch and her family and you did this thing."

"I don't care!" screamed Blue Snow, struggling to break free from the old one's grasp. "Let me go!"

The old one squeezed Blue Snow's shoulder. But he was not angry. He jerked the boy to his feet but behind his roughness he was gentle and sad.

"You hate me! You're like all the others! They hate me! They all hate me! I hate you! I hate you!"

"Walk," said the old one, pushing the boy, kicking and struggling, in front of him. "We will talk later when we are where we must go."

"Where are you taking me?" cried the boy as the old man led him up the mountain, away from the village.

The old one did not answer. They walked until the darkness closed about them, the boy fighting to be free, but the old one was strong beyond his years and held him firmly.

"You are strong, old one."

"It is not my power that moves me. Keep walking. You cannot escape."

As the way became dark for the going, the old one led, dragging the boy behind him. He neither turned aside nor hesitated. It was as if he saw as well in the dark as in the day.

All night they traveled and far into the next day. The boy grew hungry and tired but the old man was unmoved by his pleas and seemed to grow neither tired nor hungry himself.

They reached the valley of the Aomi when the sun was at its highest in the sky.

Blue Snow looked upon the valley with dark fears growing through his shoulders and legs. A sickness and a chill came upon him and his teeth touched ice in his mouth. A cold wind and the smell of old things in the ground blew in his face.

"What is this place?" asked Blue Snow.

"This is the valley of Aomi. And there, coming alive in the rocks, is Aomi." The old one pointed and a bright but dull thing rattled upon the rocks. It rose and it slithered and it rolled and its shape changed. It grew and it went little and it was a small animal and it was part of the ground and the wind across the grass and insects whirring up in summer.

It flew like a bird and it went whipping along like a black snake and it did not move at all and it got closer and stayed where it lay, a demon trapped in the rocks.

Suddenly it became a rabbit and it hopped across Blue Snow's feet, dragging a lame leg.

"Catch it and kill it," suddenly cried the old one, with a strange, terrible voice that commanded.

And forgetting everything, Blue Snow chased the crippled one across the ground. He forgot who he was. His fears were forgotten in the run of the chase as he smashed at the rabbit with a rock. His face was hot with a fever and a wildness. And he struck again and again and his muscles raced with the good feelings that swam in his blood.

The rabbit, its head smashed into jelly, boiled over and became a small bird fluttering across the ground with a broken wing.

"Kill it!" commanded the old one.

Again Blue Snow gave chase, battering the bird down, crushing its frail body in his hands. The bird poured out of his hands and became a fawn without eyes and Blue Snow sank his teeth into the fawn's neck, seeking the jugular, loving the blood taste and the animal heat. And the old man stood and watched and Aomi died many times.

And the valley of Aomi filled with the excited hunger of the chase and the quick snap of torment and death. Finally, exhausted with blood and hate, Blue Snow lay on his back.

The old one stood above him, not smiling. His face was grim and filled with the wisdom of one who asks questions that are not mysteries.

"You cannot leave here now. You must stay."

Blue Snow sat up, his breath coming in gasps. "I will leave anytime I like."

The old one shook his head. "There is no way out for you until there is no hate left in you."

"I do not understand. I want to go home," said Blue Snow.

"You use empty words. You are home. Aomi, the demon, is your home."

"Why me?" cried Blue Snow. "Why was I chosen for the demon?"

"Because you chose," said the old one. "I watched you. I watched the children play cruel games upon each other as children do. But you were different. You are the kind that goes deeper than the cruelty of small ones. You are a killer whose inside is rotten with hate like a dead tree. And because your kind never tires of hating and hurting, you are here."

"I want to leave! I am frightened! I don't want to stay with the demon."

"Aomi eats kindness. He cannot harm you. There is not a kind bone in your body. The beast demon will give you all you need. Eat of Aomi's flesh for hunger, drink his blood for thirst. All that you love is here. For Aomi can be tormented a thousand ways and never die. Go. Aomi awaits the chase, the feel of death snapping its jaws. Use your hate. Go. Aomi grows restless. Give Aomi the pain it hates and loves. Hate is the love that is not a weak pain. Only the strong fight demons." And the old one pointed to the flowing strength of Aomi gathering upon the ground.

"How long will I stay? How long will I do this, old one?" asked Blue Snow, feeling the fever rising in him again, tearing him away from the questions that tumbled in his brain.

"Until you become gray like me and dried out with the fever and the hating. Who can say how long that will be?"

"How will I know when it is time to stop?" said Blue Snow, his body alive and trembling with the fever and the wildness.

"You will know neither a hunger nor a thirst that Aomi will not fill. You will live a long time but when the hating stops you will stop. You will know when the hating stops, just as I knew when my time to stop had come. For you see, I was once the Aomi's keeper."

"Because you hated?" asked Blue Snow and then he was gone, forgetting the question, no longer seeing the old one or living in the outside world. Blue Snow only saw the quick coming and flowing of the demon Aomi. And he killed and killed and the old one was forgotten.

"No," said the old one, talking to himself as he watched with sad, knowing eyes. "No," said the old one, the rustling leaf that blows gently and crumbles. "Because I could not love."

WHEN THEY GO AWAY

Horseboy digging in the yard, digging in the dust. No grass in the yard, lot of dust there.

"What you doing?" yells his old lady grandmother. "You like dog buried a bone?"

"Digging," says Horseboy, "just digging."

"What for digging?" ask Grandmother.

"Just," he says, "just digging."

"Crazy you," she say. "You all the time dig for the hell of it?"

Horseboy dump out one last coffee can of dirt and climb out of hole. Hole maybe two feet deep. Hole not going anywhere, just hole.

"You want eat fore you go?" she say and she rub her arms with her hands like they ache. She got that crying look in her face.

"I ain't hungry." He is not looking at her face. Like maybe the sun on her white hair so bright it hurts his eyes.

"You hungry," she say, "but it not food you hungry for."

He look up at her, ashamed, but his back stiffen up and there is more pride there in that back of his than is shame. And she know that. She know that boy is got pride.

"Come into the house and I fix you some deer meat. Some stew. Come in now, mind, I fix for you one time more."

"You know I ain't hungry," he says and he scruffs his old boots along edge of hole. He is hate this good-bye.

"Just think, Horseboy, just think, think this, come same time next day you be miles gone. Gone be all them miles away and nobody fix you stew. Nobody fix for you."

She bend over with stiff, hurting old back and brush hair off of his face. He lets her do it but he feel too grown-up for her doing that.

"Maybe I eat just a little," says Horseboy, knowing it make her happy if he do it.

So the old lady smile, crooked teeth and all, and put her arm around him and they walk back inside and that hole in the ground, ain't nothing, just a hole back there.

He's sitting down in front of that beat-up old table his uncle found at the dump. He's sitting there and she fixing for him and she talk. "You ain't bother to go leave us? Leave your grandmother and where your father and mother buried, buried right here behind the house and you ain't bother going? Where you be not having your peoples?" say the old woman, waving her finger at him. "This reservation here, maybe you don't care about your peoples no more?"

"I care," he say and his face look hurting. There is a rat, under the floor by the table, making noise and Horseboy listening to that rat moving down there like it important. He trying not to look at the old lady and listening, that rat there, yes, rat.

The old lady comes away from the old woodstove with a pot, walking careful like so she don't step in that hole in the floor Horseboy never got around fixing. The steam rises up off that stew, smelling good. She set it down on the table in front of Horseboy and dishes out some in an old cracked bowl for him. Horseboy is looking away.

"Don't your belly hurt inside thinking how you going away? What about Nila? What about Nila girl? Don't you hurt in the belly?" The old lady won't let up on him.

"I get there on a wage and soonest time I'm sending for

Nila. Send for you Grandmother. This ain't a fit living place," says Horseboy.

"I was here born and here die," says the old woman. "I don't give damn all time talking about wage."

"Well, not me," say Horseboy. "Not this one. I want to see places."

"What places?" she ask.

"I don't know. Just places."

"You just like that Brokeshoulder, that Leon Brokeshoulder. Off to fight in that damn Vietnams. What for he doing that? Who am them Vietnams? I ask you who they am. Ain't they brownskin like us and living on land like our fathers and we over there killing them short brownskin peoples. Why for we do that?"

"For America," says Horseboy. "It was done for America."

"Oh, that's lie. A lie and you knowing it. Them brownskin peoples like us Indians. They never do us harm. What right that Leon Brokeshoulder got leaving reservation and going over there killing peoples never hurt him?"

"It's different when you're in Army," says Horseboy. "You have to do what they tell you."

"If they tell you jump off mountain, if they tell you swallow glass, you fool enough and do it? Ain't that the way of it?"

Horseboy push away from the table, disgusted, almost knocking wobbly old table over. "Aw, you don't understand nothing. You just so old, old woman, and things has passed you by. Things is different now."

The old lady wave her bony fist in his face. "You respect your elders!"

Horseboy look at her, sharp, kind of sad, not so angry; then ashamed, he look away. "Sorry," he mutter.

"Ain't you gone eat?"

"Not hungry now," says Horseboy.

The old woman pushed the steaming bowl of deer stew closer to him on the table. "Where you get food like that? Only word food you gone hear when you leave here is hamburger. Crazy white man and his hamburger, you mind what I say. You eat this once so you remember what eating good is."

Horseboy pull himself reluctantly back to the table and stir the stew listlessly with a fork. He less hungry now than before. He eats a biteful anyway, just 'cause she watching.

There was a knock on the old screen door and Leon Brokeshoulder was leaning against the screen. Resting. "Car's ready. Got the transmission fixed," he says.

Horseboy look up and wave him in. He come through the door slowly and awkwardly. The artificial leg of his never seemed to fit him just right.

He come into the kitchen and pull up a chair beside Horseboy. Leon was painfully thin, his thick black hair cut close to his scalp, in military fashion. He had a broad scar across his forehead as wide as a zipper. Stepping on a land mine in Nam had really mess him up.

"How you feeling boy? You look death," says the old woman and she came around behind him and felt his ribs through his shirt. "Hungry? I got deer stew."

"I just ate," says Leon, dragging a crumpled pack of cigarettes out of his shirt pocket.

She put a bowl of deer stew in front of him anyway. "Well eat again skeleton or wind gone think you tumbleweed and blowing you away."

Leon, being polite, eat a little, but he isn't hungry much.

"They was a wreck down along Pine Canyon. Remember Joseph Eagle from over to Schoonerton?"

Horseboy grunt.

"Well, they say his pickup truck went off crazy like at the

top of the turn and went down the cliff with him. Pieces of him scattered all over Pine Canyon."

"Drunk?" asks Horseboy, knowing Joseph Eagle.

"Stinking with it," says Leon. "You ever know him not to be stinking with it. All the time drunk, that one."

"Yeah," says Horseboy, who had gotten drunk with Joseph Eagle a couple times himself.

"You ready to leave?" asks Leon and then Nila comes into the room through the back door. Nila with the shoes that hurts her in that restaurant down the way she works at.

"Why he going?" says the old lady. "You tell me, Leon Brokeshoulder, why this boy gots to go so far and away. Tell me why this boy going away?"

Nila open her eyes wide at that and lean wearylike in that doorway. There is sweat in her face from the long walk, but the way her face is made up, she stop at home before she wander along down here to see Horseboy.

"Where you going away, Horseboy? Where are you going?" ask Nila, rubbing her hands nervously on her waitress dress.

"Away," says Horseboy, not looking at her. "To a city, I guess, maybe Austin or maybe up to Denver, Colorado."

"No good. No good," says the old lady. "You don't know your heart, you don't . . ."

"You leave me be," says Horseboy. "I ain't go there for fun. I ain't go there for a good time and that's all. I looking for a job there . . . steady work . . . a good wage. I can't stay here no more. I don't want end like Joseph Eagle, drunk all the time and so stinking not knowing you killed yourself."

"You gone leave being Indian then," says his old lady grandmother. "What you are wanting is not Indian, not Indian."

"I can't help it. If it takes that, that is what is," say Horseboy.

Leon has turned his back to the table, looking out the screen door past Nila's head. He is embarrass to hear this that goes on.

Nila comes in and sets at the table across from Horseboy. She sits in the chair, uncomfortable, that waitress dress too tight on her, other things too.

The old lady comes around the table to offer her something to eat.

"Nila," she say, noticing how that girl is looking, "what you done to your hair? What you done to eyes? What is eye blackness? Sick, maybe? Work too much, maybe?"

"I just cut hair, is all, like white girls at work cut it. Too hot in restaurant for long hair. Eye stuff is makeup; all the white girls at restaurant wearing it now."

"Shame," say the old lady. "You not proud of the face Great Spirit gave you, putting that white man's stuff on, shame. Cutting hair like them white women's. Think Horseboy like you better that way?"

"I never think of it," say Nila, but she has, and she looks over at Horseboy. Horseboy is still busy not looking at her.

"Do you like hair cut this way, Horseboy?"

Horseboy looks over at Nila but it is hard for him to answer her question. He just shrugs and then look away again.

Leon gets up, favoring his leg and looks around, like he is ready to go.

Horseboy gets up too.

They move over to the door, fast, like they trying to escape.

The old lady pokes Nila in the shoulder. Nila is kind of just sitting there, staring at the old table. "Can't there some way you stop this foolishness. Can't there some way you keep this boy from going?" say the old lady.

Nila shake her head no, not lifting her eyes. "If he wants to go, let him. It is his life." Still staring at that table.

Horseboy been looking at her out of corner of his eye and

when he hears her say that, his shoulders sink a little and he
turn to the door and open it.

Horseboy and Leon go out the door and then Horseboy
stops and look back through the screen door.

"You got a white girl, don't you?" says the old lady, looking at Horseboy through the screen in that clever way she
have when she find the truth in things.

"Yes," say Horseboy very softly. "In Austin."

"Gone marry her?" ask Nila, holding back tears.

"Maybe," say Horseboy and then he turns and is gone,
him and Leon is gone and in their car and going away.

Nila and the old lady silent there for a while and then
Nila run to the door and shout through the screen. "I'll
scratch her eyes out!"

But her words only reach out through the dust of the car
as it leaves and fall like wingless birds in that hole Horseboy
was digging.

Nila stand there and her hands reach up there, feeling
where all that hair used to be. She touch the corners of
her eyes and the black makeup comes away on her fingers.
Then, then the tears start.

The old lady comes over to her and puts her arm around
her shoulders. "Once my daughter, Sky, went and cut her
hair for a man. He went off and married white then any-
ways, thought he wasn't Indian no more, like that. Horseboy
don't be knowing this. Joseph Eagle was name of that mans.
White woman leave him, so he come back here Indian, die
Indian, even if couldn't live Indian."

"I cut my hair for him," say Nila, crying. "I thought he
would like it."

"You ain't stop being Indian, hair ain't stop growing. It get
long again. It don't matter. It don't matter, mind what I say,
you just be true what you are, be Indian." The old lady give
her a hug and Nila just against her, crying soft on her shoul-

der. "You hush crying up now. You lucky to be knowing who you are. Horseboy ain't learn that yet."

"But I love him," cries Nila.

"And he loving you," says the old lady, "and he be back, you wait see, back before hair all get long again."

"Do you really think he be back?" ask Nila, hope on her face.

"Sure," lie the old lady, looking away from Nila's face, "they always come back."

WHO WAS THE FIRST OSCAR
TO WIN A NEGRO?

No help from the audience, please!

The tour guide pulled the curtain aside. The tour members waved their antennae with astonishment. Peter Renoir was removing his clothes. He looked up startled as he heard the shower curtain rustle. He saw the aliens staring at him from the bathtub.

"You will note the clothes that bind, the jaws that snap," said Raffi the tour guide. "Also you will note," continued Raffi, "the accouterments which denote that this culture limits tactile communication."

"Communication with the self by masturbation is no doubt universal," suggested a little Koapa.

"I note that he is rather pale, so unlike the black one we saw last week," said a larger Koapa.

"Visual identification," said the tour guide. "Who to avoid and what not to touch."

"What keeps them from becoming universally poignant, a heart-throb for the galaxy?" asked the little Koapa. "They seem so frail, so tragic."

"It has no appreciation of sculpture for one thing," said the tour guide. "There are social restraints against touching art objects, for another."

"How would it feel if we touched it?" asked the little Koapa, carving himself into a beautiful hand.

"Better not," said the tour guide. "They are used to the illusion of separating art from life. We might confuse it."

Peter Renoir fainted dead away.

"You see," lectured the tour guide, "we've already confused it."

"Is it dead?" asked the little Koapa, forming into a golden stream of tears.

"No," said the tour guide, speaking from experience. "It is simply experiencing self-criticism."

In the fall of 1939 Benito Mussolini condemned the Marx Brothers and ordered his subjects not to laugh at them.

"Somehow," said Semina, letting the bathrobe fall at her feet, "it just doesn't seem real this way."

Renoir turned out the room lights, pulled the window drapes closed. He moved in beside her and said, "Perhaps it will seem more real this way." His hand reached out and hit the switch. The projector whirred and the screen burst into color. Renoir appeared naked on the screen. Semina moved in beside him and let her bathrobe fall at her feet. He dragged her down on the waterbed and together as the camera tilted and zoomed in, they reached for squishy delight. The film clattered along, the leader winding off the spool and beating madly against the projector housing.

Semina sighed and took Renoir's hand off her knee. "It seemed so much more real that way, didn't it?"

"Yes," said Renoir, folding his hands in his lap. "It was realer than real. Let's watch it again instead."

A film critic peeping through the keyhole said, "The camera thrusts us into the depth of things."

Realism was too easy. The movies offered themselves as substitutes. The American woman watches film to learn how to become a better female impersonator.

FROM: Peter Renoir
SUBJECT: Rewrite of "Who Was the First Oscar to Win a Negro?"

Obviously this one can't wait. Let's dump the jerk who wrote it and get one of our people on it. We don't want to blow this one. How about we give it to Sam Bernardino. You remember him. He's the one who did that TV quickie about the attack of giant roaches or was it chickens? Let's get a Screen Guild member on this for Christ Sakes! What we're talking about here is our survival!

Peter Renoir, Producer

"Must you always think like a marshal? Can't you think like a human being just once?" Semina wept openly on the set of her latest movie.

Her five-year-old son, not to be upstaged, pointed at the Marshal's gun and said, quite distinctly, "Daddy!"

"You can take it up your movie," said the alien, holding Lillian Gish in his extended forepaws. "I been sitting in the front row for twenty-seven silent years and I'll be damned if my baby is going to talk!"

"Damn you, damn your naked eyes!" cursed Peter Renoir. "We can't afford a transition like this! Not now! We were just learning how to talk with our eyes and now we are being interrupted by sound!"

"Peter!" breathed Semina. "The cheers! The shouting!"

"It's nineteen hundred and thirty," he said. "And I've had fourteen lovers and want you to bring back the Auk."

FROM A LETTER WRITTEN IN THE FUTURE:

The guarantee against limits is a sense of alternatives. Back in Oregon, I dreamed all my life of being the Bank of California. We lived across from the debtors' prison. I used to sit in the darkest of theaters and watch the light and shadow. I was hypnotized by Marilyn Monroe and a known associate of the Seven Dwarfs. I was hypnotized, the dreams provided. Did I dream of being me instead?

I turned in a fire one day, after letting it burn for a while to make sure it was a good one, and got my name in the newspaper. Later, I became convinced that people were so blank, so destroyed, that no mad scientist was ever necessary to destroy their souls.

Perhaps everything terrible is something that wants to help me. Perhaps it is only that other people's fantasies have nothing to do with reality.

Vonda McIntyre

P.S.: "Remember the night we met and I lost my glass slipper?"

"Yes," he said, low angle, soft focus, violins beginning.

"That was when I discovered my existence was insufficiently interesting."

The director screamed *cut* after the word *existence* and turned to his assistant and said, "Print it, it's a wrap."

Peter Renoir was an alien and didn't know any better. He came here for a good education. A good sex education. He was an alien and didn't know any better. He turned to television for advice, for the facts, for the inside info. He found what he sought. He never had a minute of regret.

"It could have happened to anyone," he said. And indeed he might just have been right. He was an alien and he came here from another galaxy, came here with a problem of sorts. It was the kind of thing that can happen to anybody. The people on Peter Renoir's planet, they had this culture, see, really a ball-breaker, see, with everything wired for sound, juiced right up to the limits. See, they had perfected perfection. They had it made, only they were so busy being perfect, they forgot how to do it.

"What do you mean, DO IT?"

"I mean do it, DO IT," said Peter Renoir. "It's a natural."

Semina scratched inelegantly. "It'll never sell product," she said.

"Oh, man!" shouted Peter Renoir. "You cannot see the frigging unbelievable scope of this thing! I mean, see, he comes eight million miles or whatever in this big frigging flying space something or other! See what I'm getting at?"

"Jesus!" said Semina. "That's a hell of a long drive for just one person. Don't he let somebody else take a turn driving?"

"That's what I'm getting at!" shouted Peter Renoir. "See him and his girl, course she looks just like a real girl like on TV or something. You know, what was the name of that broad with the gaps in her teeth, you know the one on the acne commercial, the before one?"

"Norma Jean, you mean," said Semina, finally catching some of his enthusiasm.

"See, they got the hots, they got 'em so bad and they don't know which end is which."

"Right!" screamed Semina. "And that's where we hit them with the commercial, our plug for toilet paper!"

"Aw, shit," said Peter Renoir, "you should of let me say it first! You're always taking all the fun out of it!"

I know he's out there. I know he's reading my story, wondering about the size of my breasts, missing every single word of what I had to say. How many times have I told him. Explore other people's metaphors. It isn't only a metaphor. It's an angle of vision.

I've based my life on the theory of the persistence of vision. You can't throw up three thousand years of art in three minutes and not see something.

Joanna Russ

"Jesus!" said Peter Renoir. "That name, Joanna Russ. Sounds very Hollywood. I think we can go with it. I really think this one is our baby. How does she look in a bikini?"

I am an alchemist, the father of science, the death of us all. I am the real root of science. I am an erotic science. I am deeply involved with buried aspects of reality, from novel to film and back again.

Rain is copulation. The sexual activity of man is an energy-to-matter conversion. Mineral formations are sexual crystal trysts. The creation of the world was a sexual activity. I am an alchemist. I can remember love affairs of chemicals and stars, romances of stones, fertility in fire. I am an alchemist.

On the other hand, maybe I am only showing you the soft underbelly of a stealing tide of nostalgia. Maybe I need a new analogy.

I am a science-fiction writer, the mother impregnator of dreams. I reflect culture. Culture reflects me. Why are both these statements true?

"Joanna Russ, and we throw in some other kind of broad, I don't know who just yet, but we tear her clothes halfway off and so she's got to look like she's asking for it, but what I mean we can maybe do," said Peter Renoir, "is have these two broads, see, and this alien menace from somewhere, how the hell I know, one of the damn planets or something. Are you with me on this?"

"Gotcha," said Semina, licking the end of her pencil and scribbling it down on her napkin.

"Well see, my idea for the series is first these two aliens come down and these two broads have one hell of a time trying to escape from them. In the last ten minutes of the show, we burn this Russ's clothes off, see, get some good leg shots going for us and maybe a couple good back shots, then the alien catches her and rapes the hell out of her. We make that nine minutes and then cut away for the commercial. We cut back for the final minute, in which it is revealed that the alien is really working for the government. So the show ends on an upbeat note and we sell one hell of a lot of product."

"But won't it get stale? Don't you have to have a sad show once in a while, you know a downbeat one for a change of pace?" asked Semina.

"You mean like could we add something like a pet goat or something that gets killed off or a baby dog or something?" asked Peter Renoir, mulling it over in his head.

His face lit up. "Oh, man! It just hit me! It's a frigging natural! We come back next week and throw in this time machine device, see, and she and this other broad gets thrown back into the past. Back to fifteen hundred and forty-eight or whenever the hell the Civil War was. Do you see it! See, we have the whole Confederate Army and the Union Army and Russ and this other broad lands in a Union town. We kill off the other broad when the Rebels overrun the town. Then, see, we got the audience's sympathy. We got their attention and then the Confederate Army catches Joanna Russ and rapes the hell out of her. We do it in three versions, soft focus for television with lots of shots of horses taken extra so we can cut them in, crotch closeups for the drive-in and for the big downtown theater market, we got to shoot something symbolic or something. I don't know what, maybe a picture of Orson Welles in the buff."

"It's going to be beautiful," said Semina.

"Then see, the way we end it is, the Union Army comes in and saves her."

"Then what happens?" asked Semina.

"Then the Union Army rapes the hell out of her and the picture ends and we are left with a sense of loss."

"You're a frigging genius!" said Semina. "You really are, Peter."

"Oh, it was nothing," said Peter Renoir. "But it damn well will sell."

NOTE TO THE READER: I'LL BET THE EDITOR THINKS I DON'T CARE TOO MUCH FOR YOU. HE'S WRONG. PLEASE REMEMBER THE EDITOR BEHIND HIS SMILE IS MY PIMP. I DO LOVE YOU VERY DEARLY AT EXACTLY FIVE CENTS A WORD. AND BECAUSE I LOVE YOU, I'M GOING TO CLARIFY THINGS FOR YOU. I WANT EVERYTHING IN THIS STORY TO BE RIGHT BETWEEN US.

ON PLOTTING THE STORY:

The plot is simply about an alien who has come into your bedroom, your life, your church. He has come seeking knowledge, information. He is looking to the reader for that information. He is an alien and doesn't care how he gets it. He wants information about doing it. Yes, he does. He is an alien and he learned about your planet from watching television and going to the drive-in movies on Saturday and Sunday nights. While the alien is very much in sympathy with the reader, while the alien is very much on the reader's side, the alien cannot deny his personal feelings and values as an alien, which is why his meaning may not be too clear. This is the story of his struggle in your world to figure out how to do it.

In 1934 Clark Gable took off his shirt and underneath he wasn't wearing an undershirt. The undershirt industry fell off that year by 50 percent.

"Christ!" said Peter Renoir. "When is this damn story going to finish up? I say we cut the hell out of the son of a bitching thing. I say we muzzle the son of a bitch and get it over with. He isn't Screen Guild anyway. Just because he wrote some stuff under the name of Rudyard Kipling do I have to listen to the whole thing? I got things to do."

"But how the hell we going to do it up without you got the whole picture?"

"I got the picture," said Peter Renoir. "We take out Gunga Din and substitute Nanette Fabray. Don't tell me I ain't got the picture!"

"Who we gonna get to direct it?"

"How about we get Gower Champion? I want someone who isn't going to mess it up by knowing anything."

"You're a genius, Peter Renoir," said Semina.

"Yes, I know," said Peter Renoir.

Semina tells a lie and then tells the truth. There is no change in her face. She murders a stripper named Shirley who wants to get married and have a baby. She murders a stripper who is not named Shirley and who doesn't want to get married and would sell a baby if she could get anything out of it. There is no change in her face.

She goes away for the weekend with a bowling team sponsored by a local carwash. The inbuilt demand for a higher standard of living creates a feeling of menace. The captain of the bowling team dies from heart failure that may or may not have been caused by the bullet in his brain. Panic-stricken by this turn of events, she decides to escape from this world. She buys a ticket and enters a movie house to watch a double feature. The film ends and we are left with a sense of familiarity.

Peter Renoir is an alien. He feels naked without his clothes. He equates morality with being uncomfortable. If only he were illiterate. We could save him if he were illiterate. The ways of official literacy do not equip people to know themselves, the past or the present.

Why doesn't Peter Renoir understand as we understand? Why doesn't he know the world has been conquered? Don't you understand? The world has been conquered. What have they done to the earth and the people?

Who are they? I can explain me. I am a creature of the nightland. I am of the soil. I am people. That is who I am.

Who are they? They are technology. They are the aliens. Technology is the creature of the conquered world. The world, all my peoples, is the materials of technology, not its form.

The car did not do the work of the horse. It replaced it. Technology will not do the work of the people. It will replace them.

Semina is arrested for flaunting antisexual implications. Peter Renoir bails her out. They fall in love. They build it up to a severe emotional disturbance. However, as they realize that they are at last approaching a permanence and security unknown to them and their generation, Peter Renoir finds himself pursuing anticliché to anticlimax.

Semina catches him kissing himself. He defends himself by casually remarking, "When sex dies it is climax."

She snubs him in the closing scene by proclaiming, "Others may call you sensibly adaptive but I think you are a faggot."

The movie ends and we are left without a sense.

"Semina," said Peter Renoir, moving toward her in a zoom, up angle. "Why don't we do it?"

"You mean, uh, oh dearest!" said Semina. "You've finally discovered the secret! After millions of miles and one of your smiles, you've finally found out how to do it. I'm so proud of you!"

"Aw, shucks," said Peter Renoir, blushing. "It wasn't nothing special. I just watched television until I found out how they did it."

"Nevertheless," said Semina, "I'm impressed. How do we do it?"

"Well," said Peter Renoir, blushing through every pore. "I believe the best way is for you to prop yourself up on that couch over there. Kind of slouch around and blink your eyes a lot. Then light up a cigarette."

"Then what?" pole-vaulted Semina, arching enthusiastically over his every word.

"Then," said Peter Renoir, with dramatic emphasis and a slight snigger, "I leap on top of you, your hand will become limp and the cigarette will drop to the floor. Later you will cry."

"Why don't we just forget the whole thing?" said Semina.

I am an sf fanzine editor. I am forty-nine years old and never have been kissed. I am a peeping tom, a chronic masturbator. The mirror is my staff of life, my totem, my life's work. The window is my prey. What is my threat? What is my power?

My secret is that I am lonely and in that silence that surrounds me, I am able to pierce the windows with my mouth and make an unknowing partner of anyone in my eyes' range. I am deeply involved in a current fan project to cure blindness with a whore's spittle. My threat and my power is in my ability to motivate, to "show the donkey the carrot."

MUTATIONS ARE ONLY POSSIBLE THE MOMENT ONE GOES FROM ONE SET OF CONVENTIONS TO ANOTHER.

The science-fiction editor, in order to play his game with a full deck, is forced to accept only images that represent an orderly sequence. An image path that is familiar. That is why science fiction sometimes repeats itself itself itself itself itself itself itself and why this story will get thirty-five rejection slips. An Indian tells the story of his life from the day the world began. He will never tell his life's story with any regard to chronology. He may work back or work forward or both. He will repeat himself many times and omit things frequently. Shall I apologize for this pagan mysticism, the willful obscurity about my craft? I want to withhold my skills from profane onlookers. I am, after all, repeating the works of nature.

Peter Renoir and Semina are hopelessly in love and they decide to kill each other. While on a visit to Renoir's mother they decide to kill Mommy instead. Before they can carry it out, however, a semi-pro football team, turned cannibal after losing their league franchise, attacks the house. Peter Renoir is killed, as is his mother. Semina helps them eat the evidence of their intellectual dilemma, nearly choking on Renoir's mother, who is tough and stringy. She joins the team as an outside linebacker. She is later benched and then raped by a referee. The film ends in a closeup on the fifty-yard line and we are left with a sense of loss.

From *Reviews in Film:*

Only a director of the stature of Peter Renoir could bring himself so consistently to face contemporary reality. The determination to show only what is real is clearly an aspect of Renoir's wider determination to expose himself completely to the age in which we live. The scene in which an apple is stuffed up Peter Renoir's anus in preparation for being butchered, cooked and eaten is an obvious attempt to tell us that what we are watching is more than a film but instead the very framework of everyday reality. At the end of the film, when the director allows us to actually see one of the corpses breathing, we are once again assured in the director's unshakable faith in the unconquerorable human spirit.

Peter Renoir is leaving his rich wife because he is too comfortable. Semina is leaving Richmond, Indiana, because she is tired of sleeping with truck drivers. They meet and fall in love beside a tennis-ball factory. Semina is kidnapped on the first night they spend together by one of her old truck-driver friends. Peter Renoir pursues her the length and breadth of highway 101. He finds the semi-truck in which she was a prisoner. The truck is empty with the exception of the corpse of a midget named Russell.

He finally catches up with them in the men's room of a truck stop in New Jersey. He realizes that he has lost her because the truck driver is built better. Peter climbs to the top of a ten-story building and dives off. Nine floors later he repents of his rash action but alas, too late. The movie ends and we are left with a sense of having seen it.

HOW YOU, THE READER, CAN APPRECIATE THIS STORY.

Begin like this. You the reader, somewhat awkward at first, begin reading this story with as much intelligence and sensibility as you can bring to it. In the passages where the theme (animal suffering) is most acute, you will be at least able to note the technique and methodology by which parts of the effect were achieved. But when the theme weakens, you will find yourself with a surplus of attention which you can profitably direct toward some other activity.

Preferably some quiet and fatal activity.

"I've got it for sure, this time," said Peter Renoir.

Semina rolled her eyes. "I'll see it first before I believe it. What do we do?"

"Well, we drop all our clothes on the floor and then we get under the sheets of the bed and we talk. Then I get up and go for a drive in my sports car. Later you will cry."

"Is that it?"

"There's more," said Peter Renoir.

"Such as?"

"Well," said Peter Renoir with a smile. "Then the Army comes in and rapes the hell out of both of us."

"It's just like a movie," said Semina and she was deeply moved by it. It almost made her want to cry but she held it in. She wasn't scheduled to cry until the next scene.

Now, class, why is this story worth studying?

Because it is metaphor as metamorphosis. It has become a story cut off from its name, habits, associations. Detached, it sees everything and nothing. It sees all things, swirling independently and then becoming gradually connected. The change of detachment. I am talking to you personally, because detached I become only a thing, an exercise, a creation, an amusement. I become the thing, in and of itself. It is disintegration into pure existence, and at that point, I the thing, I the writer, I the reason for this story, I all of these things, am free to become endlessly anything.

A literary critic peeping through the keyhole said, "The storm over style and content will rage forever."

Peter Renoir and Semina are trapped in an outhouse by two Dominican friars and several very irate forest rangers. Violence seems imminent. The priests are chanting, "We are only interested in the superficial."

The forest rangers break down the door. The rangers make off with Semina, the priests disappear into the night with Peter Renoir. Semina reveals her pregnancy by word association and the rangers take her deep into the woods. They rape her and we are left with a sense of guilt. Peter Renoir is castrated in a frustrated rape attempt. We are left with a sense of accomplishment.

EVERY WORLD
WITH A STRING ATTACHED

I don't see what you see. I see what I see. You see the city
and your lips put that name to it. It is a CITY. I see a
severed insect mound.

Your green earth is my ocean. My eyes are my body. The
ability to see is a viral infection. Do you have the cure?

The CITY is an architectural ring of disease with sex at its
center. The CITY. The genitals of the angry CITY have
been sedated with suburbs. But let us suppose a journey, let
us bring forth one of the diseased creatures from a dollar
hotel. Let us bring him forth and send him to the edge of
the city where he shall discover muddied dreams and zones
of sophisticated boredom. We will point the eyes of the city
through his eyes and we shall hear the city speaking. It will
say, "Look where we worship. Look where we worship."

I am the diseased creature from a dollar hotel. I have
fulfilled the premises inherent in life. I have predicted the
future. Cancel my subscription to the RESURRECTION. I
have predicted the future.

Suppose I saw a foot cut off from its body. Suppose I saw
it. If I looked downward, immediately realizing that it was
not my foot, if I looked downward and discovered the foot
belonged to someone else, would I not be curious?

Curiosity is the greatest single impregnator of mothers in
the universe. Even a person of my ability is not immune to
it. I would tap the foot lightly. It would seem inanimate. It

would seem reluctant to strike up a conversation. It would be dead.

Perhaps it will be severed from a visually unpleasing pulp which lies beneath the bed of an overturned truck. Perhaps.

By itself, the foot will have a curiously appealing quality to it. It will give off an aura of continental largesse that will please me greatly. I will immediately desire its acquaintance.

That is my prediction of the future. It came true. I did see just such a foot. I think I saw it on Tuesday.

Using one of my less desirable skills, I animated the foot and gave it the power of speech. The foot took it quite well. It wiggled its toes experimentally, opened its arches and cleared its metatarsals, preparatory to speaking. Outwardly, it seemed quite pleased with my ministrations.

"Shall we walk and talk?" I began.

"Let's," said the foot. "But keep in mind that neither of us should smile or light up a cigarette."

"I accept your limitations," I said and I began walking briskly down the long hot highway. The foot fell into step with me and we continued along in thoughtful silence.

"I suppose you've walked this way before?" I finally asked.

"Yes and no," said the foot, somewhat cryptically.

"I am a former sky swallower," I said, by way of introduction.

"And I am a foot," said the foot, arching its toes in a little bow, bending stiffly at the joints. "I am still employed as such, although bereft of my employer. It seems, thanks to you, I am yet a foot but am now, thankfully, self-employed."

"It was my pleasure," I replied. "It seemed the least I could do."

Without warning, the foot suddenly rammed into an object, stubbing all of its toes. It cried out in pain and hopped up and down.

"Perhaps I should have given you eyes too," I observed. "This could have been avoided."

"What the hell did I trip over?"

I bent over, as moved by curiosity as the foot seemed to be, and immediately noted that it seemed to be a string made out of rock. It was either that or a rock made out of string.

"It seems to be a string."

"And to what is it attached?" inquired the foot. "To what does it lead?"

"To those questions, I am afraid I draw a blank. It seems to be of indeterminate length, stretching off as far as the eye can see."

"Perhaps we should follow it," suggested the foot.

The suggestion was agreeable to me and we set out to follow the string. Let us suppose a journey.

We journeyed many days and nights. It seemed to stretch out undiminished before us like a fat man climbing a light-year. The string stretched ahead of us, turning, twisting like a nightmare, and we followed patiently.

In Germany, it led through a large oven, as big as a house, that reeked faintly of gas. The string was coiled around a factory that made walls in Berlin. In France, the string covered the ground in cobwebs beneath guillotines.

In America, the string was used to tie the knots that held the doors of slaughterhouses closed against the public. In America, the string tied itself into colored worlds that said, "You can't eat here. You can't sleep here. You can't marry my sister."

We diligently followed the string. In Georgia, the string was a tightrope that political candidates swallowed and unswallowed with arthritic grace.

In Canada, the string was woven up in tuberculous-infected blankets that the Hudson Bay Company passed out to Indians.

In South Dakota, the string was a lynch rope that kept the mice from seeing the cat.

In South America, the string became a highway that mowed down the grass that hid tiny statues made out of wind and night. In South America, the string was a ribbon that rich people cut that let the first car drive across the broken bodies of dying animals, dying dreams.

Patiently, we followed the string.

In Spain, the string was a cure for venereal disease the natives called the INQUISITION. Everyone the string touched was ultimately cured when the grass grew back over their bodies.

In Florida, the string was a roll of tickets to the alligator farm where the last of the Seminoles lived off tips tourists gave him when he put his head inside of an alligator's jaws. He put his head inside and prayed the alligator would swallow.

In Nebraska, the string was a rosary that a Catholic priest tied to a dead Indian baby. In Nebraska, the string was a rosary that built two churches for every child, with the financial support of a God who ultimately said, "I can't see your face in my mind."

We followed the string, ceaselessly. It weaved its way through the bloodstreams of men and women, carelessly draped around their loins in curling spirals of mistrust and doubt. We followed the string. In some men, it entered their eyes and filled the empty sockets with frayed rope. In some women, it entered their bellies as umbilical cords that fed them, that took nourishment from the blood of the children.

As we traveled, we felt less inclined toward conversation, for stretched before us were the visual puppets of the world that danced on string.

It was endlessly fascinating, and we were speechless before the vast panorama of the never-ending string. How it curled like a twisted whore, screaming and thrashing like a child—a small child in nightmare alley! And the string touched all things and beauty and death and hate and love were all knots on the endless surface of the string, all there from the cruelty of children to the kindness of men who killed cattle with hammers in slaughterhouses.

We grew weary. We had seen too much and, perhaps, felt too little.

"I grow weary," I said and I looked with longing once more at the sky and dreamed of the days when I once held it like candy in my mouth.

"I too am weary," said the foot. "I have walked too far and feel that I have blisters that make my mortality significant and valuable."

"Blisters in themselves are no sign of accomplishment," I admonished the foot. "There has yet to be a world that did not have a string attached. There has yet to be a world, but one can hope for it. Until then, we must pay attention that we see more clearly the string so that we may someday touch people without tying them to us like beaded souvenirs on a necklace."

The foot thought this over carefully for a little while, as I once more aimed myself like an arrow of longing at the sky. All my thoughts had turned to the change of seasons, to the harmony of the sky and the four winds of the creation.

"What do you think of Western Civilization?" asked the foot.

I pulled the edge of a cloud out of my mouth long enough to shout back down at him, "I think it would be a very good idea!"

WHY HAS THE VIRGIN MARY
NEVER ENTERED
THE WIGWAM OF
STANDING BEAR?

If you want to get to heaven, you got to raise a little hell.
If you want to know how the future is, the old ones know it
is wrapped within the skins of the beginning. It is there or
there is no future. I have been writing that everywhere. On
trees, flywings, and people rising to the objection. On your
enemies you shall write your name. That is how it is written.
I am a proud woman. I am a warrior and a chief and I walk
everywhere. As a woman, I have lately found the sun very
hot on my head and it has made me feel that I was in the
fire. These are not the old times. These are the times of the
fire.

And so it is I come into this place, poised like a great
question of beginnings on the edge of the future. And so it is
I have come into this valley and drunk of these waters, these
waters in the metal bowls of buildings with colored windows. I think they call this kind of building a church. They
call this water "holy water," but if the truth be known, it
doesn't taste very good. I suspect someone has washed his
head in it.

I have traveled through time with the memory of better
times and better feelings. I have only quite recently been
saved. I can't remember what I have been saved from, but

the missionary tells me I have been saved. Actually, I was only thirsty for water. If the white people have crucified Jesus Christ, let them punish themselves. Our men and women had nothing to do with it. If he had come among us, we would have treated him better.

I have come to this place from a great height to find the religiously secure. I've heard they have them here and I thought I would come here and see one. A man without doubt is no man at all and so I have come a great distance to see one. I have lived a long time and my mind has been filled with a fear and a dread. They say God has a beard. I have heard much talk of this and I am filled with fear and dread. I have heard much talk of this in my lodge, far from the pinball machines of the whites, about the Immaculate Conception. It must have been quite an event, to judge by the fuss.

Personally, I do not see what all the shooting and shouting is about. After two thousand years, I think it no longer important how clean someone was when they did it. If the child was born on a clean sheet, it is nothing to shout about. I myself was born on a new buffalo robe and you do not find me yelling about it.

Why I am speaking today on this matter is that I think I have been fooled. Fooled and shamed by treachery. I think the white people have fooled me into thinking that they came from this world. I think they have shamed me into thinking I am less than what I am. I think the white people fell out of some giant animal's udder. I think they crawled out of a crack in a lizard's skin. The reason I think I have been fooled I shall relate to you in the story of Standing Bear who, against my advice, went to the beginning of the world. It is this place from which all people came into this world. It is this place from which we draw all our wisdom. It was I who gave advice to Standing Bear. I said, "Don't go where it whoops." It is wrong to go there alone.

Standing Bear was sliding up and down a tree at the bottom, trying to itch at the places where the tree scratched him. He was always a walking-backward man. He often nocked the arrow before stringing the bow.

A woman in a car came along the road beside the tree. He watched her go by. She did not stop. This gave him an idea. Later he forgot it.

He stopped scratching himself and this gave him another idea. He thought perhaps he would go to the place where the world began. Nobody had ever done that as far as he knew. There had never been a need for it, he thought to himself. If there had been, he was sure he would find a long line to buy tickets. (The lines are long and we women see them now, but as we push into the future, no one will be buying tickets.)

So he went back to his lodge and packed his bag. He put the bag under the bed where no one would step on it and wandered away into the woods to find the place where the world began. He was a great one for wandering off into the woods on his own. But he had to rely on other people to find him afterward. Sometimes this worked out and sometimes it didn't.

I am a proud woman. Once the Cherokee nation followed me into battle. I happened to meet him as he entered the forest. I was out in the woods early that morning. I was looking for my place in the forest of the god they say wears a beard. I was looking for my place. They tell me my place is sitting on a thistle bush, composing a warning to people who make obscene phone calls. My warning was, "PERHAPS WE WILL EVEN GET TO LIKE IT BY AND BY."

He blinked at me as if surprised to see me. Sometimes surprise turns into terror. I could see it in his face. I said, "Fortuitous and most cogent it is, our meeting at such a propitious time in such an auspicious place." How cleverly I had been disguised!

Standing Bear replied, "Blow less boldly in the talk of old
white men's horse whistle. If your ear offends him, he will
pluck you and pluck you and thus it will ever be."

"Only for money," was my reply. "They wouldn't understand it any other way."

"I am off to see the place where the world began," said
Standing Bear. "Will you follow me?"

"Why dawdle in the bathroom? My advice is, don't go
where it whoops. Don't go if you expect me to follow you."

"I will need help, for the way is hard and long and they
do not have bus service there, I think. Will you come with
me?"

I untucked my buckskin face and checked my schedule.
The only alternative was coming out with a modern contra-
ceptive for men. So I would go to help but not to follow. I
agreed to go.

And go we did. We glided across the glide spots, we whistled through the whistle spots. We walked across the water,
we tiptoed through the torpedoes. As we went we remembered how simple it used to be. There was no one to blame
in the old days. We only had to say the sun did it. Now the
beginning was poised on the edge of the future and we had
lost so much. Life does not rise easy under the shadow of
death.

As we walked we discussed the universals, the things of
importance in our lives, all those things once the playthings
of healthy children now suggested for mature audiences
only. We reflected sadly on the family jewels, we talked at
leisure of a week's worth in one little bag. It was automatic.
It was unsupported by committee votes. It was strong stuff
and people grew out of it and took comfort out of it and
strength. No one sold tickets or waited in lines. It was strong
stuff, never weak. Ah, those were the days, we reflected. We
were wise enough to know then what were the strongest
weapons, the hardest weapons in any fight. Who has not

heard the sound of sex on skin? But in the land of the bowls in buildings with colored windows, they taught people how to fall away. And now a thing of beauty is a foul ball forever. Such is life. It shall not always be such at the beginning, at the edge of the future.

"We've come a long way, baby," said Standing Bear, but as he spoke his gaze fell in the direction he had come.

"I cannot scurry around holding a book between my knees," I said. "I can only hitch my horse to the wind and hope the people do not fall away."

"You are a philosopher," said Standing Bear. "That is not good. People will expect you to use peyote."

"I have been driven soft and slow with a new language. I see women killed like pets you've just begun to name," I said, and as we approached the place where the world began, my feelings grew stronger. I stretched the wings of my hands over my eyes, and birdlike, my eyes crawled away from the world to look in at me. And my feelings grew stronger. It is always thus at the edge of the future. I found my hands bruised by lace and unnatural delicacy, felt my hands melting into a fistful of silence. And I knew that strong feeling and I said, "I have felt the breech birth of cultures clashing."

"And is there an end to it?" asked Standing Bear.

I smiled and said, "You can tell when it's over. When it's done with you, it lets out a little cry of triumph (BEEP!) and then runs to take a PSSSSSSST furtively up your sleeve. Who among us has not known the white man's love? Who has not felt the great TWINKLE TWINKLE of laps and knees?"

"You are a philosopher and a thinker," said Standing Bear. "It is not too good. People will expect you use drugs. Or think you mad."

Our journey continued as we moved without moving. Suddenly, I gave a great cry. "Let us talk no more of what others think! Do you not see before you the place where the world began?"

Standing Bear closed his eyes without making a sound. The world closes its eyes without a sound. Sometimes the world thinks this will make things go away. He said, "I grow weary of this sport. I cannot look at what I can see. It is too visible. It is the mystery in life that makes it sweet." As he spoke thus, a tiny hand caught him by the throat and pulled him away from the edge of the future. Life is easy without tomorrow and the truth shrinks.

I could not agree. The moment I saw the place where the world began, I was seized with knowing what it meant. You think it'll never happen to you. I studied it and turned to look at the white man looking over my shoulder. He had my wire tangled. There are always white men looking over my shoulder. Without them, who could plug me into the nearest wall outlet? I turned and said to him, "I know you are dying to get in there and push."

"Flameless heat is pure comfort," he agreed.

"I find no flicker of hope in your heat. It has not helped my golf game. It has not improved my life. Besides, I was never really afraid that some night in the summer, perhaps at 2 A.M., I'd wish I had the GREAT INDOORS."

"But no man wants the same thing every night," said the white man. "Unless he is a judge of creativity and has a format."

Standing Bear fell back toward the edge of the future as laughter came from his belly and pushed him. He said, "Who has not heard a silly white woman say, 'My man likes something unexpected now and then. That's why I serve him a tremendous bang.'" And Standing Bear laughed. And laughter was a place beside the edge of the future.

I drew my warrior's robes about me. I arranged sunrise and sunset very carefully around me. I am a proud woman and I walk everywhere. I said, "At the beginning of the world is the beginning of the way. Have we not come to start over? And this time here at the edge of the future, will we not set the world right? I am a proud woman and I walk everywhere, as was our way."

"Pride comes before a fall," said the white man, but he made a treaty face and he vanished without a trace. His words ate him alive.

"I laugh at rattlesnake clothes. I eat the apple of life with pride. The world was the white man's body. White men killed it every twenty-eight days. They are too selfish. At the edge of the future, here in this god, we shall twist it away from your weak fingers."

The white man moved after death, but it was too late. The connection was made. I was plugged into the outlet, the image danced on the screen, but it was too late. If he feasted at the edge of the electric fire, he himself was spit on his own ribs, turning slowly in the sun. It was too late.

"Woman!" he yelled at me, offering products with his eyes. "It is not right that you evade the great undress."

I spat on him. I hit in the center of his TV screen. I am the chief, the warrior who killed High Hefner. I killed him very poetically. I gave him the most beautiful body a girl ever had. It was his own. How he shrieked when his hips went in and his chest went out. I spat on the white man. He melted into the air I breathe. At the beginning of the world it is written that none may follow, that all must walk beside each other.

Woman is strength and wisdom. That was the beginning of the world. And the only world that ever lived never lived without this beginning. And this is the edge of the future.

"Standing Bear!" cried the ghost of the white man, reaching to drag another after him, reaching to pull him down into the past after the beginning. "Are you a man or a mouse? Will you let this woman get away with . . ."

But Standing Bear had no time to tell him coochie-coo

and tickle his fat baby chin. He was a man walking with a woman. Both knew what it is to follow, both knew what it is to lead. He was a man walking with a woman. What more can I say he might have said to the white man? Bill me later, he might have said, talking to the white man in the only way he can understand.

I am a woman. I sang at the beginning of the world. We will sing at the end. There will be bloodshed. Throats will be cut by strong hands when the music dies. But we will all be in one place at the edge of the future.

The voices heard at the beginning are those of strong men and strong women. The voices that will be heard at the end are those of strong men and strong women. If you take pride in lies you believe about yourself, if you feel better being self-deceived, stay in the present. Don't go where it whoops. The war cry will only make you equal. It will only thrust you over the edge of the future.

I am a proud woman. I walk everywhere. I have heard rumors that the God who lives in bowls in buildings with colored windows wears a beard. I know it's a lie.

I thank God by thanking myself.

YOUR CRUEL FACE

You take some cops, they punch in, do their job, punch out, and that's it. Not me. When I punch into the computer, I come alive. I hate punching out. Man, the next wombcop practically has to pry me out. I got this, like, obsession. I love my work. If I could work two straight shifts, I would. I love it that much.

Like tonight, I tool in and plunk myself into the console web. The console monitors sweep into position as the street monitors flip back into my patrol sector. There's my sector. Nothing else exists for me when I slam my rump into the chair. The audio helmet fits over my head and my hands fit the twin trigger grips of my double bank of pocket lasers. My mobile units begin their random sweeps.

Not a minute in the chair and already the action is on.

"POSITION" says the computer. "PICKUP 10, MONITOR 7."

I flip the right toggles. The mobile unit zeros in. Hit the wide angle scoop. There in the left of the screen, a man. Punch in zoom lens. Closeup. Enlarge. Print and file.

The computer reads out, "CAUCASOID, MALE, INTOXICA-TION, PUBLIC, URINATION IN PUBLIC. Scan . . . video . . . 234-56-3456-6 . . . TAYLOR, WILLIAM PAUL . . . PRIOR . . . 1 COUNT 432 . . . 5 COUNTS . . . 433."

I whistle. Six misdemeanors. That's the limit. I push the red code and wait. Central hits the line ten seconds later.

"COMMAND DECISION." They are telling me, not asking me.

"Destroy," I decide. Six misdemeanors make him habitual. I line in my mobile unit, trigger off a burst, and the man explodes in flame. Quick, efficient. No waste. Total burn-down. Now it's Sanitation's problem.

Central is still on the line. I read in the report. "Decision to terminate. Executed."

"GOOD WORK." Central rings off. I punch in file tapes and code it for termination. I attach the 314 code to the tape which automatically notifies Sanitation of the termination. A clean job. Makes a man feel useful.

Monitor 13 is showing a blank wall. Something wrong here. I run my eyes over the monitor consoles. No wonder—the last wombcop unplugged my audio cables on sector 13. Stupid greenie. Probably using the plug-in to clean his fingernails with. Takes all kinds.

I run in the sector 13 plug-in. Suddenly the blank wall makes sense. House number in the corner of the screen. Audio homes in on a family dispute. A gun goes off. Antici-pate is the name of the game. Before I even plug in the audio hookup, I have a troubleshooter unit on the way. An-other shot and then my audio goes right off the deep end. Sound of lasers blowing in metal doors. Video switchover. Man and woman. Woman dead, man with gun. Homicide, il-legal possession of hand weapon.

No need to punch it up for me. Instant execution. Filed and verified by Central. Routine situation when we catch them in the act. It's the little criminals that give us the trou-ble. We can't always burn them down on the spot. The big ones are the easy ones—total burndowns and no busy-work punching up their files. It's better that way. A cop shouldn't have to mess with too much tape work. Let the computers handle it.

Computers are a cop's dream come true. A wombcop like myself can patrol a hundred city blocks for an eight-hour shift. God, when you think of the waste the way they used to do it. And all that legal nonsense that used to turn crimi-nals loose. None of that kind of thing now. We catch the criminal in the act and his videotape is all the trial we need. And wombcops like myself are all the judges we need. We don't pamper criminals. We make short work of them around here.

"POSITION," the computer clacks. I punch in monitor 6. It's a female, Negroid. Walking past the monitor. Out of range. I punch in. Curfew violation.

"Follow and detain."

Mobile unit moves forward, scanners set on her. Tape beginning to file. I punch in audio.

"Stop." My voice sounds good booming through the mobile unit's big speakers. Usually that one word is enough. Not this time. She keeps walking. The mobile unit flashes the emergency panel. My console lights up. Sector 7 queries, "ASSISTANCE?" I delay. I repeat the message. "Stop. This is Mobile Unit 6. You are ordered to stop. Failure to stop will be considered resisting arrest."

She must be made out of stone. She hasn't looked around once and she's picked up her pace. Monitor 7 lights up as Mobile Unit 7 moves into sector 6 on an intercept pattern.

"Stop. This is Wombcop Stevens. Stop. This is a direct order." What the hell is wrong with her anyway? Is she trying to get burned down? This time I damn near yell it at her. "Stop!"

She just keeps walking.

"You dumb whore!" I curse, forgetting that the linkup to the mobile unit is still on.

It's over in a flash. Total burndown. I panic. Punch up the data. What a screwup! They just burn her down for prostitution on my say-so! I punch in some questions. I get this horrible suspicion. Like maybe the woman was deaf?

The computer reads out, "NEGROID . . . FEMALE . . . 234-84-3722-4 . . . WILLIS, MARY LENA . . . DIRECTOR . . . POLICE UNITY LEAGUE . . . HANDICAP . . . DEAF. NO ARREST, NO CONVICTIONS."

That tears it. What to do? I punch a quick hold on the filing of the tape. A temporary solution at best. This is going to be a real stinker. I've got to think my way out of this. Hell, no way. They'll dock my pay for a week at least.

What will be, will be. Have to get back to work. Send it in, file it, forget it. Make the next shot clean. These things happen. Can't let it sour me on this job. I love my work.

The buzzer rings. It's time for my break. I punch in the automatics and sit back for a smoke and a tube of coffee-chew. I flip the learning module down in front of me and settle back into the chair for a little cramming. The screen flips on. I punch in a random number. My idea of relaxation is studying police methods. Like I say, I love my work.

The learning module comes on with a program on criminal facial characteristics. A series of mug shots, typical faces of thugs and murderers. Interesting. A footnote suggests criminal composite studies. I punch in the coordinates. A face forms on the screen. The face on the viewer, says the tape, is that of a demented killer, chosen from the files as the criminal facial type most often replicated.

I study the face. Code letters that identify it are not criminal codes. Pity the poor guy, some slob private citizen who's got the perfect example of a criminal face. I'd hate to be in his shoes. God, that guy looks familiar. Think I knew someone like that back in school. My curiosity gets the better of me.

Mug shots hardly ever look like the real tapes of a guy. Everybody knows that. Just for the hell of it, I punch in his code, ask for identification tapes. Be interesting to know what the man with criminal facial characteristics does for a living. It'a a police-file code and not an identity code.

The computer reads out, "WORKING . . . RESTRICTED . . . PUBLIC SERVANT . . . DELAY . . . DELAY."

That figures, and I have to laugh. With the perfect criminal face, what else but a public servant? The computer hooks in with Central to get an OK on the check. Central opens a line to me. I have to identify myself. "Wombcop 345-45 Stevens, Roger Davis, security clearance, code 298-76."

"CONFIRMED AND CLEARED." Central goes off the line.

The computer opens up monitor 4 and the audio goes up automatically. I hook in and wait. The screen bursts into life. God! Who has the perfect face of a killer?

"WOMBCOP 345-45 STEVENS, ROGER DAVIS," clacks the computer.

JUST LIKE GENE AUTRY:
A FOXTROT
A CHEROKEE VERSION
OF JESUS CHRIST
ENTERING OUR LIVES

I was once in love with Jesus Christ. It didn't work out like everybody thought it would, but I did learn something from the experience. Experience. I learned that there is an antidote to losing at love, perhaps winning at sex. I say "Perhaps" because I don't mean "Evidently." (Sex is a properly organized two-car funeral.)

My only complaint was that Jesus Christ didn't love me back. There was something cold and alien about her. She was always trying to get me to go back to the reservation and see what was being held in reserve. She was always winking at hoods and vice with versa. She didn't love me, but she insisted that I should love her out of anything like false modesty. (She often said she was chosen to play the part of Jesus Christ because it was type casting.)

Throughout the entire affair, between the entrances and the exits (of which there were several), there was only one tragic flaw in an otherwise perfect scenario. She just plain didn't love me back. She didn't love me and that was a cure and a caution. It was a cure for which there is no disease and it can be fatal. Whole tribes have caught the cure and died out. I couldn't let that happen to me. My legs would

never stand for it. I don't mind dying. I just don't want to
die out.

It wasn't a question of faith because I know my own
mind. I've read about my mind extensively. I know how it
functions. I know exactly what it's thinking even when it
isn't. I can prove I know how my mind works by citing an
example of a time when it did work. For instance, although
I was deep in the lap of love with Jesus Christ, I was still ra-
tional enough to cancel my subscription to the resurrection.
I had a subscription and a program book because I made
the mistake of briefly belonging to the church of my choice.

Shall I tell you how I came to belong to the church of my
choice and tell you who chose it for me?

I was born in Wounded Knee, South Dakota, population
thirty-seven. Wounded Knee has twenty-four buildings.
Twelve and one half of those buildings are churches. Perhaps you will be fascinated by the statistical one half? (You
amuse too easily.) Why not call it thirteen unlucky churches
and let it go at that?

It's a long story. It is. It has something to do with good
and something to do with evil. Good and Evil. It has something to do with the forces of darkness and something to do
with the forces of light. Them too. Perhaps I should skip it.
I want to talk about Jesus Christ. Why clutter up the discus-
sion with inessentials?

Jesus Christ, whom I first met in the summer of 1968 (it
was a bad year for everybody) on a back road in New Mexico, has, being the Jesus Christ that Jesus Christ is Jesus
Christ of, always fascinated me. Always. I regard Jesus
Christ in the same light and with the same regard one usually reserves for amputated arms, decapitated heads, and dis-
emboweled children. There is, if you follow me, a certain
something about Jesus Christ. Call it charm, call it high-
pressure hype, call it venereal disease, what do I care what

you call it. I am me (and I have been more so, lately) and what you call it has nothing to do with it.

How did I fall in love with Jesus Christ? What first attracted me to her? I rolled rocks in front of her tourist eyes and three days later, like an especially virulent, Sunday Afternoon Radio Gospel Swing Time Jubilee United Revival Fires Jumping Kilowatt. (I only get to breathe in the parentheses) 100 Percent All Singing, 100 Percent All Talking, 100 Percent All Dancing, 100 Percent All Shouting, Yelling and Foaming at the Mouth, I Believe It Lordy, Indeed I do, Jesus Christ, she pulled the leeches of her love off her arms and came swarming out of the radio-station cave like the motel owner who discovered I really had fifteen naked Puerto Ricans hidden in the trunk of my car, some of them women and all of them children.

I could simplify this by simply saying she fell out of the sky and crashed through the roof of my outhouse but somehow, telling it like that, just doesn't seem dignified. It has the personal touch, I admit; but, somehow, out of a God you always expect something a little more flashy. You always expect a little more out of a God. If God passes air, one expects it will be essentially, operatic. Perhaps a cantata from Lohengrin. If God picks his nose, one will expect it to be Enrico Fermi and the cyclotron, goosing atoms like chorus girls and having a high old time on an atomic scale. With God you expect more and always get too much. Something like that.

I had a hard time at first believing she was real. Mainly because Jesus Christ had this way of wearing her nose tilted at an angle so she could look down it at people who didn't know her. If anyone would have asked me, I would have told them she had a fake nose. (You can forgive anything in a God but a tendency to dress up in lampshades and wear false noses.) She was real enough, though, of that there was little doubt. Her presence *had* been prophesied. We pretty much figured she'd be along, by and by. The prophecy said and I quote, "Things are gone hell and gone get worse, by and by."

And sure enough, she showed up. You can't tell me there's nothing in this business of prophecy. I've seen it work. Oh there were intimations, to be sure; there were hints scattered around. You almost had to buy tickets in advance in order to get a seat. We'd seen her footprints (size thirteen, triple A) all over Plymouth Rock (and we scrubbed and scrubbed and we still couldn't get those footprints out. We wore our little cleaning arrows down to the feathers and the footprints still wouldn't come out. She had *big* feet and they really sunk in deep).

She came riding up in a kiddie car, whooping and hollering like a two-dollar drunk in front of a five-and-dime. Her fenders were shiny, made of prefabricated martyrs, and she got a lot of miles to the Spanish galleon. We recognized her right away. (The ones who didn't, died.) She stood out like a pregnant whore in a male police lineup. She carried her breasts in her hip pocket like either the old rugged cross or a pocket flask. (Like all religious stories, we are open to interpretation. Or as the scholars would say, if forced to tell the truth, what happened is anybody's guess.)

Jesus Christ was lurid with limbs, liberalism, and Daddy's car. She had a sick headache and always walked with her legs crossed. She was also full of five-by-six publicity glossies but I was able to overlook that shortcoming because of my great love for her. After all, this was my red zoo and she seemed sincere about everything being everything (what a sweet-tongued promiser she was) and when you're in love, the whole world is a tourist attraction. She was the tourist and I was attracted. We spoke to each other at first, exclusively with our crotches. We didn't mean to get so deeply religious like that right off the bagatelle but that's life. Or is it? I forget which it is. I may not know what is but I know quite a lot about what isn't. And, socially, I've met all the people who shouldn't be.

Which myth brought her to the reservation that week, of all weeks? Was it sexually linked with the Protestant work ethic? Did it make me spin in the grave years before I am buried? Did it center on Geronimo and body contact with horses? Perhaps I will never know. Maybe I will never care one way or the other either. (Was it to dispel the rumors that Billy Graham doesn't have a swivel to blow anything out of and that his mouth works as a food substitute?)

I don't want you to think I hate her, that I'd like to take a contract out on Jesus Christ. It's true I did sleep with her once but I'm not the type who carries grudges. Besides, personal degradations and hoof and mouth roll off my back like oil spill off a seabird's back. Besides I've been insulted by professionals and one night of harmful vapor and frantic bending down on your knees (the worst position in the Kama Sutra for ethnic minorities) isn't enough to get a rise out of me. I worked at it, gave it a thought or two, but it's hard to hate a girl, a woman, who, for a fat woman, perspired less than any other fat girl, fat woman I ever knew. I mean that as a compliment. (The only one I'll ever give her.)

If she had hit her head more often, if she had let it hang out the window when she was driving her car. If insects had smashed into her mouth, I would have loved her more; I would have found her a better place to park.

Being in her presence was ultimately frustrating. It was like being aware of Custer's funeral, a hundred years too late to attend and a hundred years too soon to take a stand, saying, "Though unable to attend, I would like to leave word that I approve." It was like successfully training a mad dog to bite by choice not chance and then discovering that all your enemies had died in an eclipse of the moon so thorough it registered 11 on the Richter scale. It was like being a

turkey at Thanksgiving and having to be so stuffed with
thankfulness that it hurt right down to the bone. It was like
brotherhood, hugging infectious lepers and kissing cancer
sores.

Jesus Christ was the kind of woman who wanted to be everywhere and everything to everybody. (She slept around is
what I'm trying to say.) Her feet were so big she could fast-
talk you into anything with them. (The old jokes have it
that the red stuff between her toes was slow Indians.) She
was overwhelming and she almost overwhelmed me. I admit
it, I was almost compromised. On me, with the chains, lynch
ropes, and beaded castration complexes, she tried harder.
She gave me the deluxe, the Jesus Christ with everything
on it and anchovies. I mean, she was all over me with true-
pieces-of-the-cross fingernails, but I never let her into my
bathroom. I may have slept with her, I may have mounted
her for Lent, but I never let her into my bathroom. (If you
do not sense a victory on my part at this point in this narrative, I will have to.)

I've put up with a lot. Yes, I have. I've put up with the
white man's Indian-land fetish (the I-Can't-Get-To-Sleep-
Unless-I-Have-Indian-Land-Under-My-Pillow   bit.)   I've
moved gracefully wherever I was told to move. But I draw
the line at the bathroom. Any movements I make in the
bathroom are strictly my own. I'm not here to do motion
study on your bowel movements, I'm here to move mine. To
do it as my ancestors have done it before me (and sometimes behind me and off to the left a lot, now that I think of
it. It was always best to do it downwind).

I didn't complain when Jesus Christ sang six choruses of
the NEW YORK *TIMES* REVIEW OF BOOKS FIGHT
SONG in the sacred sun altar. I kept my peace when her
brother, down from Harvard for a weekend, bought FIRST
AMERICAN SERIAL RIGHTS on my sister, but I broke
her camera when she followed me into the bathroom.

I had told her over and over again that I didn't mind the coming of Jesus Christ as long as she left us with our own silverware when she left and didn't wipe her hands on the toilet seats. I wouldn't have cared one way or the other, if she wanted to have a second coming, if she'd stayed out of the bathroom when I was in. I kept telling her, while I'm in there, I prefer to worship Jesus Christ sitting down by myself. (You have to keep something sacred.)

No matter how long I sat in there, religiously straining in her name, no matter how exclusive I tried to be about her, she always got in somehow. She oozed through the walls like a secret blessing. Her presence was more deeply felt, indeed seemed much more natural, in the bathroom than on any other place on the reservation.

Her eyes seemed to genuflect from the bottom of the sink. Often we heard her laughter harmonizing with the gurgle of the toilet. The flush went deep into the earth on a gush, so cross your heart and hope to die, the plumbing seemed blessed. The stool reminded me of you, Miss Jesus Christ, as a lover. The plumbing, the beads of condescension on the pipes, the wisecracks in the bathroom tile, the essence of all these things dripped you, yes, you. Miss Jesus Christ. You were busted and disgusted and put away wet.

As a lover, Jesus went at it as if there were no tomorrow and, what's worse, often as if there were no yesterday either. It kept me pregnant and happy and in the kitchen. It kept me constantly defused. I could never tell if I was blushing or cooking. Sometimes I was both and it was my life's work. That's what Jesus said but momentarily, a narcissistic tendency in her, had mistaken me for some other sex, you know, the other sex, the one Jesus Christ created in Genesis. Jesus divided people into the good guys US and the bad thems, THEM. (PITY, PITY, I SAY. OH THEM, OH US! Did we ever really happen? Weren't we all once US and burdened with no THEM? Did we ever really happen or was it all just a dream, long ago, and faraway?)

I remember when Jesus Christ and I had our first lover's quarrel. It was on one of those days when the world is trying to be new all over again and you don't feel like wearing a shirt to church. One of those days when fishing in the creek seemed more religious than a single-breasted suit and a prayer book opened to page one. One of those days. I'd been talking to my brothers, the animals, breathing with the green things and I'd been late for the predawn mass. Jesus was infuriated. She noticed my absence when they passed around the collection plate and she was enraged. She said, using her best Sermon on Mounting voice, "If you don't love me faithfully, you'll have to go to jail where sadistic choirboys will beat your naked behind with leather whips."

I listened to this and, having thought it over carefully, I couldn't resist the chance to be a pioneer and I went. Went to jail that is. The naked choirboys were civil service employees. The leather whips were made out of chains and solitary confinement.

Jail as a means to my end was full of high culture and Christian charity. Food poisoning was one of the highest arts, but the jailer didn't do anything about it until I collapsed in the middle of the night and saw a nightmare figure riding a dead horse and cashing checks under an assumed name. It was hell there until I recognized myself.

Jesus Christ sent her love from some missile silo deep within the center of the earth. I got a complimentary Bible that was autographed by Jesus Christ personally and featured color foldouts of the sacred cities of Jerusalem and Detroit. There was also a glossary that featured a debate between two biblical scholars on the exact location where Jesus Christ, in her infinite wisdom, will give the Earth an enema on Judgment Day. Personally, I favored Pasadena since it was an already well-known parade route.

Jail made my toenails grow inward like little knives of lost meaning and dampened my eagle of freedom's enthusiasm for flying. The prison doctor, fresh from a course on refurnishing electric chairs in vinyl, was above art. He thought at first that I had a social disease which would have raised my stature among the rapists in the cellblock. But, eventually, he found out that I was imprisoned not for having a social disease but because I *didn't* have one. I had caught the cure, not the disease. When it seemed obvious to him that there wasn't going to be any money in it, the doctor went home and waited for the local funeral director to call and complain about my failure to provide him with state-supported employment.

I remember the lip's corruption, the gossip that used to vomit through the ventilator shafts and I was in there, how long, I forget. A long time, I know, and the rapists taught me card tricks and ate my food for me. I think I remember two cells and I know we had to stand on the John (the baptist) in the last cell and look through the ventilator pipes to plan our defense. When I speak of we, I am talking about Jesus Christ who went right into jail with me. She went as a guard and my lawyer. She also moonlighted as torturer and when the state could get it up enough to ever get around to doing an execution, she filled in as executioner, too. I'll say this much for Jesus Christ. She was no quitter.

I lived very low to the ground and Jesus Christ was right down there with me. She used to step on my hands with her dancing shoes when I scrubbed the floor of the cell. I kept all the hand grenades the Bible society sent underwater in the sink, and I never told her about the crazy letters I wrote to THE GREAT SPIRIT C/O SANTA'S WORKSHOP, NORTH POLE, EARTH. Sometimes I saw her riding the backs of insects that were so overwhelmed with brotherhood they came and slept in my bed with me. Sometimes.

I don't want you to think I went to jail without a trial. I

had a very nice trial. Not too gaudy, not too cheap, just a nice trial slightly reminiscent of the Spanish Inquisition (nothing like a well-developed sense of history and carrying on traditions). It was a two-part inquisition, with one part being the legal one in the courtroom and the other part that came before court. The one where they pounded all the clues out of me with nightsticks on the way to the police station.

The judge and the trial. The judge was made out of old rubber bands, and when they unplugged the air conditioner they found it was powered by 110 volts coming from his heart or something fearfully poetic like that. He was an ordained minister, a surfboard clergyman, so named for his ability to hang ten.

The trial was a jumble with three witnesses for Jesus Christ popping up like junk mail, each saying, I COMMITTED ADULTERY. After each man had given that fact away, the judge said ONE OF THESE MEN IS THE REAL MAN WHO COMMITTED ADULTERY. THE OTHER TWO ARE IMPOSTORS AND WILL TRY TO STUMP OUR PANEL OF EXPERTS. The jury asked each of the men questions and then cast dice to see who was the most likely of the three men as far as adultery goes. (Personally, I was rooting for the guy with the handbag and high heels. I had hoped he had made a breakthrough.) That was my trial. Perhaps I am confusing it with a television game show. When you fall in love with Jesus Christ and then out of it, things get confused and blur altogether. Just last week, I sat on myself, mistaking me for a chair. We blur, we blur.

My sentence was not, as the master of ceremonies had promised, two weeks in Bermuda with your choice of sins and all expenses paid. I got all the centuries expected to occur at hard labor and a recommendation for no parole, ever. It was a life sentence with the stipulation that it could be changed if they could think of something more perma-

nent. I've served two centuries already with many others of
my own kind. We blur, we blur.

Well, I'll say this much for Jesus Christ. She had me by
the short hairs for a while. She had me foxed. I didn't even
know I was living, baby. But I found out and I took it away
with me and I got my revenge on Jesus Christ. I got my revenge when the heavy, wooden beam in the building I was
knocking down, collapsed and drove an iron spike through
my shoulder.

I felt like a returning war hero (or a movie stunt man)
with all that blood pouring out of my crucifixion wound. I
didn't have my going-to-church shirt on and it was so much
better that way. All that skin showing and that enormous
hole, three inches deep, big enough to bake blackbirds in,
the doctor later said. And the blood (not of the lamb but of
the wolf) that I didn't even know I had, never expected it
was there, until I spilled it, the glorious blood! Every step I
took, my heart pumped out more blood and I knew I was
human. It was news to me. I used to know it, I guess, but
loving Jesus can make you forget the damnedest things.

That blood, my blood in a stream down my arm and
across the fingers, scarlet drops to the ground, that's what
changed me, made me see Jesus Christ as the Jesus Christ
she was the Jesus Christ of. I had been dying on the floor of
my cell, alone at night and Jesus Christ was standing just
outside the cellblock, playing five-card draw with the guy
who brought the girlie magazines, all because I didn't know
I was alive. I had been thinking about Jesus Christ, saying,
"I should have married her and saved myself from all this
grief and adopted her offspring, which seemed to be a
French Poodle named Theodore."

Under the influence of Jesus, gaily jogging through my
life in the sweatsuit she wore at Bible College, I know I
remembered thinking about wanting to reform for her sake
but my memory of that is short. My memory used to be

quite long but I cut part of it off and used it for a bookmark. I put it in the pages of a book I had been writing that said, in case somebody was watching, JESUS CHRIST I LOVE YOU AND CAN I PLEASE GO HOME. If I had reformed it would prove I hadn't really grown up yet, and never intended to. It would have meant I was turned around inside and wanted to blur. To blur, to blur. If I had reformed, it would have meant the crank I used to turn myself around inside had broken and I was stuck the way I was and would always be.

But I had been spiked, crucified, taught that pain makes its absence worthwhile when the building fell. That was the secret. The buildings have to fall and the blood has to flow and we have to go around unreformed and nobody making apologies. Because, baby, we want to know we are living.

Maybe I'm still in jail, maybe I'm still sitting in the cell, typing mechanically about all the events that happened but can't be revealed until all the cockroaches of freedom I've tied up in bandages have died with the threat of freedom on their lips. Maybe I sit here wondering how long the supply of bandages will last and whether or not (out of sight, out of mind) Miss Jesus Christ still thinks about me, wonder if she remembers the day when, well, there were so many, many days, yes so many. And the nights. Somebody ought to tell her that I can bleed. Somebody ought to tell her. I've got a down deep gut feeling that that is one thing she never knew. Never.

I used to think it funny, at night, in the cell; the circus of trying to go to sleep in the loving arms of Jesus Christ was more elevated than I ever imagined it would be. I dreamed about noble things mostly. Horse hooves and people falling off the back ends of steamboats. Canals and anthracite-coal mines. The Pope with matched luggage. Forest fires and vast fields of potato chips. I dreamed about all the people who loved Jesus Christ. These people, they disappear forever. Forever.

Just like Gene Autry: A Foxtrot. It disappears too. Jesus Christ was cowboy to my Indian. She'll disappear too. (The truth is a dude.) Licorice lights swallow up nights of cowboy and Indian fights. It's all over, the cavalry is rescuing in reverse. The horse needs new hubcaps. It's all over. The Indians are gone, the cowboys are gone, and everybody's saying it, "Gee, they don't dance like that anymore."

JUST LIKE GENE AUTRY: A FOXTROT

And Jesus Christ was buried in a shallow grave. We had to bury her because she died. The grave was shallow because she was.

Jesus Christ, daughter of virgin, son of man, no sex life to speak of, a saint, impotent like all the rest. She died of mercury poisoning. This may come as a surprise to some people. Not many because not all that many people remember who she was. And a lot of them who do remember, just plain don't believe a word of it.

How quickly they forget, we might say, if this story wasn't set in the future, the vast dim future, maybe three whole years from now, maybe ten, hardly more than that. I'd tell you the exact date but the closest I can come to imagining it is the day when all the cowboys and Indians die. The day when all the cows come home and there is nothing to come home to. (When the world throws itself up.)

How did Jesus Christ die? She got hold of a couple of loaves of bread and that's, indirectly, what killed her. How, you ask, did that kill her?

She turned those loaves into fishes, or she turned the fishes into loaves, the story is a little garbled in the translation from a nonhuman language (English) to a human one (Sonar) but, anyway, she turned out a lot of fishes. Some say she netted them, some say Jesus Christ got them by a miracle. Maybe they were rented; does it matter? As the missionaries were so fond of saying, let's not clutter this up with facts.

Let's just say she had fish all over the place. But, and this is where the death of Jesus figures in this narrative, those fish she passed out, those fish she ate and ate and ate (Jesus was quite a consumer in her time; whole cultures imitated her) were from a polluted river.

They were Jesus Christ fish, that's for sure. They had a mercury count twenty-four times higher than a safe level for human consumption. She was hardly human but she was very susceptible. Her mercury level hit seventy on the same day she felt her first foreshadowing of encroaching menopause. When her mercury count reached 289, it gave her tunnel vision and she carried that throughout her life, through all her good deeds and war crimes equally, through all her policy decisions and surprise disembowelments. Tunnel vision followed her right down into the grave and she was buried in it.

Jesus Christ spoke her own funeral oration, a speech well received by local mourners (glad to get it over with) but panned by literary critics as lacking social significance. Her last words, officially, as Jesus Christ were, "If my crown of thorns fell off, I couldn't find it unless it landed right in front of me. If it's to the left or right, I can't see it. This tunnel vision is murder."

After her death, she became a tax write-off and credit to us all. I can personally vouch for the truth of everything I have just told you. The coming of Jesus Christ into our lives was Just Like Gene Autry: A Foxtrot. It happened exactly as I say. We reported it just this way in our tribal newspaper. If you call me a liar, I will be offended.

And believe me, you don't want to offend me. I've been around. I've seen a three-headed dog at the circus. I've seen naked Japanese people through bombsite peepholes in Hiroshima. I've seen Jesus Christ. I've seen Jesus Christ and I know where all the bodies are buried.

OLD, SO VERY OLD,
AND IN THAT WISDOM,
AGELESS

They played the game, the hatred of centuries, the love of only a few moments, the never-ending dance of man and woman.

"My pretty precious," crooned the fishwoman, lips moving to mock him.

"You don't have blood in your veins, just seawater. You are blinded by old oceans," said the reptile. "You move at me on an ocean without waves. Blind. Lie with me again."

She spat at him, grinding her hips against the ballroom floor, moving to accommodate the weight of centuries.

The cold hissing caresses of the lizard dim the vision, slow the blood. The drums pick up the slow surge and rise into the air, soft wingbeats, slow animal ages.

The master of ceremonies crawled across the symbol-inscribed ballroom floor. His segmented legs rustled in the dark like dry leaves. His thin Halloween face boiled in rivulets out at them like melting tin.

"The day of the dead," whispered the dancers, bleeding from their feet. "The day of the dead."

The moon, thunder driven, careened across the sky and all the dancers moved like shadows beneath it, moved like flights of ghosts across the ballroom floor.

The reptile glittered in his shiny skin. Eyes cold with remembered ages of being, he released her. The fishwoman

fluttered away in a tattered gown. "Crystal," whispered her
shoulders as the light of the stars touched her. Her flesh
writhed against the tide of the moon. The stars. The stars
moving through her hair, writing her history in the rivers of
woman dust. Always the stars.

The reptile, rising in the dark, moves after her. His eyes
are hollow and unblinking with want and the dust drifts
across him, unchanging. Move. Motion. The legs in halting
motion, following the dust of her passing. He too dances
under the dead moon, the age-old dance. His dance stirs the
pools of blood on the floor.

The warrior king with the same tale on his lips rules in the
ancient doorways. The windows are locked shut against
morning.

The dancers, all through the long night, they whisper.
"Raven is coming! Raven is coming!" Little spider voices.
Cold stone spiders climb memory webs.

"Raven is coming!" It's written in the webs. It's written in
the blood. In the blood.

The wind blows into the room through the dead windows
and the desert comes inside and drifts across the hearts of
the dancers. The moon rules, it shrieks in the sky, and men
of the conquered night wave flags from the craters. The
world sits on a tripod and the rockets break through the skin
of the living. The sun. Where is the sun?

"This thunder shall swallow us," says the fishwoman and
she wriggles, stuck on barbed fear. The ballroom is loud
with the ocean. The dancers weave across the floor, sliding
through the blood, deepening the pools with their waning
bodies. "Bleed! Dance and bleed!" cries the fishwoman.

"Have to touch the earth, have to touch the sun," moans
the fishwoman, lashing out at the reptiles, striking back at
winter in the blood. But the moon pulls her hair in amphib-
ian circles around her face. The moon moves restlessly at the
night. The ocean is coming back.

"To dream is to look at the night and see things," whisper the dancers and they touch the wind and choke. And they touch the wind and it is dying within their breasts.

The fishwoman tears her dress away from her body and slides down into the blood. What the dancers see. She's not . . . young . . . anymore. An aged thing of flesh trapped outside a gleaming skeleton for all the time of the world. Old, so very old and in that wisdom, ageless. The bones dance within her. The ocean is in her. The stars. Always the stars.

"I promised to drown myself," cries the fishwoman to the night and the dancers move untouched beside her. The blood moves in ancient waves across the ballroom floor, pushed by the tides of the moon.

The ocean is alive with the memory of things who have crawled from the sea and learned disorder. The green hotel of life continues, stirs anew with life, life hidden in the deeps. In the deeps. The stars. Always the stars, seen from the deeps.

The blood of winged lizards moves through the burning bloodstreams of the dancers. The scorpion dances in his shadow. Fishwoman caresses the sting. It is the time when reptiles, arising, dream.

"I want to dance with you!" shrieks the Halloween man, bringing his horror face through the night. "My eyes see through the realm of pain."

His jointed legs scrape across the floor. She turns away, still dancing.

An unearthly wind moves through the room and touches the dancers. Each dancer, becomes a window, dipped in an underocean of sleep. The birds of slaughter fly in red circles above the center of the room, set free by the last dances of the world. Ice forms on the fishwoman's empty maternal shelves but she dances on. The dance. To dance until the blood goes. To dance until the world at the center of her heart stops.

The cornfields pull up the ground and shake their empty bones. The wind of the dance is almost over. It is soon finished and the rain waits to punish the bleeding wood shaped by unlasting men of the world. The rain waits. The fishwoman lies opened like a crack in the side of a mountain and the ocean drowns in her.

The dancers move restlessly against the unyielding night. Their eyes look into the dark and, dreaming, they see the shadows climbing into the strange women of the islands. The strangers and the conquered night. They see the rockets and the dying.

"Go away, easy death!" is the fishwoman's cry and the master of ceremonies, frightened by the strength in her cry, scuttles away to hide in the corners, to wait. To wait. And above, the stars, mute witnesses above the punishing world. Always the stars.

Eternal night beckons the dancers. But they dance on, unheeding. The light of day is in a big round box hidden from the eyes of men. Blackness and living death is the world being made for all but still they dance. Eternal night.

Raven is coming. Raven is coming. That is the dance. The last hope for magic. Raven is coming.

"Dance and bleed! Awaken the gods with dance and death!" cries the fishwoman.

"The day of the dead," whisper the dancers.

Raven awakes. Raven of the old times. Raven stirs in the blood of all the centuries of mankind. Raven moves, breathes! Raven from the stars. His eyes speak in secret alphabets! Hideous syllables! What does it mean? The chant? Thunder drum song. It is enough, he speaks!

"Tomorrow I enter the time of my birth. I want to be ready."

Raven is coming.

He was little and he looked up at the moon and then down and in that motion, his face became impaled on the moon. It fell on the dust plains of the moon and grew there in the rich soil of imagination and there was no getting it back.

It grew there until it covered his heart and he had no other love than the moon that had stolen his face and covered his heart. It drove him. It made him the top of his high school graduating class; it made him first at the Air Force Academy. It pushed him through rules and rituals beyond any of his kinsmen's understanding. He became a stranger among his own people. He wore no braids. He kept his hair cut short and he spent no long, learning afternoons of the summer with the old people. He saluted his superiors smartly, wore neatly pressed uniforms, and when he came home, which was seldom, all the people avoided him. He had lost his people, they all said. His heart is covered with some awful black thing and his life is cold.

His father's native tongue was lost to him and his father did not understand aerodynamics. It made his trips home pointless, embarrassing. How often a look of shame would steal across his face when he saw his father and mother, still talking of the old ways, still living by the old ways. That they shunned him mattered little.

He lived for one day and one moment. And it came to him. He was the first one of his race chosen to be an astronaut. It did not surprise him. It was a part of his plan, a necessary step in the system of his longing. He exercised, studied, flew simulated missions, endured endless rounds of tests without so much as a complaint. No questions, no doubts, no looking back, just a grim determination that ruled his life.

He took no wife, brought no children into the world. He dated women, sustained normal relationships. Part of the plan. His personality file had to show him normal. And he was normal, perfectly conditioned to it. No high periods, no low periods, a carefully regimented person.

The reporters and cameramen were there, tramping the squash, ruining the grass with their heavy cameras.

"And this is the place where it all began. And here is his father," said the commentator and he held the microphone in his father's face. "Tell me, sir, I expect you're very proud of your son?"

The old man stared, blind, into the cameras like a fish out of water.

"I no longer speak of him as my son. He is a stranger to me. He is not of our way. He is some dead man who lives in his body." That was what the old man tried to say but they switched back to the network and his words went unbroadcast as if they had never been spoken.

"Some people have no pride in anything," said the commentator, folding up the microphone cable with disgust.

Through the silence of space, the lunar module sank like a metal fist toward the surface of the moon. His eyes were blind with control. His hands moved in predetermined paths, pushing predesignated buttons. The instrumentation controlled the ship and his understanding of it was as cold and calculated a piece of instrumentation as the on-board computer was.

Touchdown was by the book, smooth, precise, no waste motion.

The dancers moved again. The wind had gone, the sounds had died. The empty moon rolled over on its back. "Raven!" cried the dancers and they moved, rising in a wave. They moved beside the ocean and the fishwoman moved with them, rose up from the blood and followed them with the dead hope. Dead hope. No. There was always the stars. The

stars. Hope would yet live, climbing valleys into the shade.
The sun come again? Raven?

The reptiles, protesting, breed impatiently beneath the
shore of the ballroom floor. "Yes, he yet lives," they cry in
anguish and they shed their skins in mourning for a reptile
age that might have been. Raven comes.

The fishwoman moves through the night, shattering the
slender rib cages of the dead with her heavy footsteps.
Across the dead valley, away from the ocean, into the frozen
light.

Just outside the airlock door, his face awaits him. The
thing that covers his heart beckons. All that he has sought
throughout his life, the answer to some mystery greater than
the life that would have trapped him had he stayed in the
village and ways of his people. He savors the moment. All of
his life, escaping his past, has been for this moment. He
depresses the door lever and there is a small snake hiss of escaping air.

His rush to step out sends him spinning down the ladder,
dangerously. The first man, the first human being to step
here! Down he moves, stepping off the last step onto the
gray soil! The first! His eyes are electrified with wonder,
with completion. No regrets, alive, no sense of loss.

The fishwoman moves down the slope of the crater. It is
true. Raven has come. She approaches unseen.

"I am the first," he shouts, filled with some terrible ec-
stasy.

She speaks. Once. And he turns to look at her, all covered
with woman dust and blood and filled with drowned oceans.
She speaks again. Softly, the almost recognizable words.

His face breaks and shrivels, crushing his heart like an
angry wave beating the shore.

She speaks again, pleading, beckoning. Why can he not understand her? The words are not his. He has never owned them.

She speaks. She begs. He falls silently into the soft soil, death in his eyes. She holds out a shield decorated with the symbol of his father's clan.

"Make us live again in you!" cries the fishwoman piteously, in words that do not touch him. And he does not take the shield from her. She falls beside him, bleeding, pulled down by lizards, and the dance is finished.

He had never learned the language or ways of his father. He could not understand her. He had lost his people.

Raven was dead.

WHEN THEY FIND YOU

It was strange and spring and the clouds did barrel rolls overhead. He awoke before dawn and went into the empty room where his waking life lived. The glassless windows brought the cool winds of the twin-moon season into the room and a chill worked into him slowly, a sleepless chill that moved through him.

He faced himself in the shaving mirror and remembered how it had been. There had been a time when he had taken pride in his aloneness, in having no people of his own kind closer than fifty miles away. But the dark-eyed young man he now faced in his mirror had been made over, had been changed by something deep and restless within him. Five years of the new world, five years living a life unfurnished with the complicated cloth of other human beings.

He rolled his tongue over his lips uneasily, disturbed by an unfamiliar taste, and his hand unconsciously strayed to his cheek in an imagined caress.

Behind the cabin, the stefel dogs moved restlessly on poison-tipped spines in the corral. They were strangely sensitive to the moods of those around them and now they shifted nervously, coiling and uncoiling spinal tendrils in flowing sheaves around their brain pouches. Their seasonal restlessness matched his own.

Gantry moved through the doorless-cabin entrance, picking up the feeding pails near the door. The metal armor on his legs clanked together as he walked. At the sound of his approach, the stefel dogs began moving together in the center of the corral. They massed their coils around a central core, forming an interwoven tube dangling into the air like a cannon barrel.

Gantry moved into the feeding shed near the corral and emerged with two pails of honey, heavily laced with potassium cyanide. The tube widened at the end as he leaned the bucket over the rail of the metal fence. The poison spines hissed through the air, beating against the fence at him. The spines bounced off his leg armor. One spine grazed the bucket, nearly hitting his hand. He jumped back with a curse, nearly dropping the bucket. The spines were instantly fatal. It was the second time in three weeks that he had come near to getting stung. I'm getting careless, he told himself; either that, or I don't care anymore.

He put the bucket back to the fence, being a little more careful where he placed his hands on the bucket this time. The tube of coiled tendrils widened even further as he poured the sweet poison down the fleshy straw the stefel dogs had formed. The honey mixture ran slowly down the tube and the blue beast began the first color change, turning a faint green as the poison began working through the cellular walls.

It took a long time for the bucket to empty and it gave him time to think. His thoughts turned to the time when he had come here. Five years ago he had been a different person and this world had been all new to him. The call for volunteers, for pioneers, had come and Gantry had been the restless type, filled with a burning itch for something different. He'd been one of the first to sign up, one of the first colonists to settle on Kingane planet and for five years he had had no regrets.

He was twenty-four when he landed, impatient of the stay-at-home life he had left on earth. He had come here hoping to rid himself forever of the settled ways of his own kind.

But in the end of his fifth year, as he tended his herd of stefel dogs under the twin moons, a dissatisfaction and a longing began in him that made his steps slow and uncertain. There was no longer any pleasure in the long stretches of Kingane summers, summers that brought the darbyo birds across the sky, circling in complicated patterns above. Beautiful creatures they were, fire red and snow white, silent like flights of dreams, wheeling like specters across the twilight skies.

But now the coming of the winter and the pebble storms oppressed him. The weather was always mild in the dead of winter and though the storms, really meteor-fragment showers, were short, it was necessary to stay inside for the two months of winter. He had faced four winters without incident, exercising daily, planning the new buildings, the stefel dog barns he knew he would someday build. But now this spring, winter yet five months away, he was already looking toward the next winter with a feeling of being trapped within himself.

He made good money, more than a man almost had a right to make. And with that money, he'd filled his empty cabin with things—amusements, books, things that occupied him for a little while. Stefel dogs, carefully tended until they reached four and one half months old and then poisoned with potassium cyanide, produced a very fine crop of nerve tissue—nerve tissue unlike human tissue in that it could regenerate. It had become the most important discovery of the five new worlds. It made him a rich man and kept the idle rich on earth very, very young. A rich man would pay plenty for a stefel-tissue transplant. The stefel tissue replaced nerve tissue, replicating the exact genetic structure and information encoded on the decaying nerve tissue it replaced. A small transplant of stefel tissue eventually replaced the entire cellular structure of a man's brain, becoming an effectual replacement immune to the ravages of time and able to regenerate itself constantly.

It was the discovery of the stefel dogs that had given man the promise of immortality. Before stefel transplants, the ability to synthesize organs had increased the life-span of man to two hundred years. They had synthetic hearts, synthetic lungs, livers, all the organs, even veins, arteries and skin. All these things had been possible because they could implant grafts taken from each of these organs and grow them in nutrient plastic, shaping them into new organs, tougher than the old ones. But the one thing beyond man's capabilities was the ability to regenerate brain and nerve tissue. They could slow down the aging process but they could not stop it entirely, not until Kingane planet opened itself to colonists and the hardy settlers discovered the stefel dogs.

The tube had filled with the honey mixture and the second color change began and Gantry watched them carefully. It was important that they not separate until he was sure they had each absorbed enough of the poison. His first year there, they had separated too quickly and the pools of nerve tissue that the stefel dogs degenerated into at death had been contaminated with unconverted brain tissue, an unpleasant experience and a very costly one. The unoxidized brain tissue began forming into crippled stefel dogs, crying piteously through their half-formed air sacs, fouling the nerve tissue with tiny synaptic runners expanded through the pools of oxidized material.

One of the tendrils near the rim of the feeding tube began fluttering, beginning to uncoil. Just narrowly missing the waving rows of poisonous spines that clattered up at him, Gantry ran his hand around the rim of the tube. His quick movement enticed the creatures into thinking that more food was coming down the tube. The tendril curled back into position as his hand made a complete circuit of the tube rim. Gantry moved his hand away, satisfied that the tendrils would stay in place long enough to allow enough poison through to complete the process.

He turned away from the creatures, absorbed in his thoughts, and walked back into the feeding shed. The sound of the generators kicking in caused a ripple in the brain-pouch fabrics of the stefel dogs. The vibration of the pump engines, which kicked on as soon as the generators had reached a sufficient level to run them, caused boil-like corrugations across the flat surfaces of the creatures' hairless bodies. The eyestalks began receding, settling into the folds of flesh above the exposed air sacs that flowed freely across the surface of the squat, now blue-gray creatures.

Gantry emerged from the building dragging a flexible length of tubing obviously connected to the machines within the interior of the feeding shed. There was a nozzle attached to the end of the hose and a thin metal tube, with a rubberoid bulb attached, dangled from a point about five inches away from the end of the tubing.

Gantry climbed over the low corral bars and moved toward the low end of the corral. The floor of the corral was made of hard-formed plastic, tilted at an angle, divided by a shallow trench around the outside of the enclosure that also bisected the middle of the corral. Mindful of the swinging poison spines reaching out toward him, Gantry inserted the hose in a groove fitted to the side of the center pool. The end of the tubing dangled into the center of the trench. He squeezed the bulb several times to force air out of the line.

Already the tube of the dogs was beginning to fold in on itself. The air sacs began sinking into the skin as the structures that held them in place began dissolving. The blood red color of the last change suffused through the dying creatures like a dying sunset. There was a hissing, melting sound and Gantry sensed a harsh, unpleasant chemical tang to the air.

It was this part of the process that had always disturbed him. It was the alienness of the creatures that bothered him. Their silence, their lack of struggle. A kind of alien intelligence that seemed in no way affected by external circumstance, yet that was sensitive to things like fear, loneliness and restlessness but contained no seeming awareness of its own destruction. At times Gantry was convinced that the creatures were humoring him, as if they were somehow above mortal considerations. Once when he had taken ill, he'd found them clustered sympathetically around the front entrance of his cabin, their poison spines folded inward inoffensively. Of course it was only his impression of them, but they seemed to radiate emotions, to be sensitive to things around them. How they had crawled out of their pen without the legs that were removed surgically at birth, he never knew. He was positive he had sensed their concern, intuited it from the waving motions of the spinal tendrils. It had been an unnerving experience, one that had remained with him for a long, long time.

For a long time after that, he had had dreams about the creatures, about them surprising him one night as he slept. Falling upon him as he slept in the night, wrapping his face up in their tendrils, covering his body in the dark with the slick, ropey nerve endings, tightening, suffocating him with their combined weight, choking him with their thick, yellow bodily excretions, flaying his body with the razor-sharp poison spines.

The first stream of oxidized nerve tissue began trickling down the narrow trench in the floor of the enclosure. It was like a semithick soup, discolored, running slowly. Gantry released the handle on the nozzle and the hose began sucking in air. Satisfied that his work was finished, he left the corral and went to the big storage tanks behind the corral. The tanks were partially full of liquid nitrogen, a perfect refrigerant for the nerve tissue that would soon be flowing into the tanks. He checked the gauges in the tanks. They were satisfactory.

The screaming began and Gantry knew it was time to leave. The screaming was not really unpleasant. It was rather melodious, a sort of birdlike trill as the air sacs began disintegrating but still he knew it for what it was, the death rattle of the creatures and he was in no mood to listen to that. He moved away from the cabin, heading down the hill toward the sulphur water spring.

A family of Riyall was there before him. The Riyall were the native race of Kingane—strange, aloof peoples, divided into many different tribes. There were very few of them left. Diseases, unknown to Kingane before the coming of Earth people, had taken whole groups of them. And then there had been fighting when many of the more highly civilized of the wild Riyalls had put up a fight against the encroachments of their land. The first year Gantry had set down on Kingane he'd signed up in the militia, had engaged in several skirmishes with the revolting Riyall bands, and had personally killed several of them. He neither liked nor disliked them. They were humanoid, so genetically close to humans, that it only required minor genetic surgery to make intermarriage possible. A thing that some of the settlers had been doing, as the loneliness of a world without women of their own kind weighed heavily upon them. It was not until his third year, that the danger was really over. The last of the big Riyall bands had been exterminated in his third year, leaving him free to spend all his time raising stefel dogs and building a small empire on the new world. Even now, there were occasional incidents, cases where travelers had been found dead, horribly disfigured by the Riyalls.

It was, therefore, with some caution that he advanced toward the spring. He had left the house without his hand weapons. He had long since stopped wearing a gun, the long years of peace seemingly canceling the need for it.

They were aware of his coming, had been a minute before he was aware that they were even there. It was a big family group, one of the largest he'd seen in the last year or so. There were about thirty adults, a dozen or so young children, and a good-sized group of teenaged youngsters. The group moved away from the water hole as he approached, falling silently back as he reached the spring.

Gantry raised his hand and drew one finger across his bared teeth. It was the sign that meant he came in peace. He moved down by the spring. They stared at him silently, expressionlessly as he cupped his hands in the water and drank his fill from the sulphurous water.

Suddenly, as if they had all reached the same decision, they moved back toward the water, careful to maintain a guarded distance between themselves and Gantry. Gantry sat back on his heels and watched them drinking, filling their lizard-bladder containers with water from the spring. They were uninhibited peoples, both sexes stripping their animal-hide clothes off to slide into the water of the spring. Having decided to ignore him, the young ones were already playing and splashing in the water.

Gantry watched them, watched as even the old ones got caught up in a water-splashing fight. And he envied them. They were simple people, always moving, rather childlike in their ways. The sight of a gray-haired old woman, naked as the day of her birth, splashing water like a five-year-old child, filled him with a kind of vicarious pleasure and, at the same time, a feeling that he was being left out.

His eyes appraised them. They were short, wiry people, about five foot eight on the average. They had white skin running to a very dark reddish-yellow. There seemed to be a great deal of variety from one group to the next. Some groups, like the one before him, had orange hair mixed with black. A strange coloration he found not at all displeasing. Their faces were basically human with the exception that facial expressions were not possible. Their faces were flat-planed. They could neither smile nor frown, lacking the facial muscles for either task. Neither could they close their eyelids nor dilate their eyes. Their eyes were the most disturbing feature. They had twin pupils, only one of which functioned in the day, while both functioned in the dark. They had a way of staring, enhanced by their lack of facial expressions and their lidless eyes, that was unnerving.

They dressed plainly, wearing cured animal hides, mostly that of the snowfur lizards that lived in the mountain regions, although, occasionally, one would have a shirt made of darbyo skin, ornately beaded with darbyo bones. Their only weakness seemed to be for shiny metal which they pounded into bracelets, items highly prized by the Riyall as having magic properties that would aid the wearer.

Then, too, they had a fondness for alcohol, a fondness that led them to great misfortune since the Riyall did not have the proper enzymes to ingest alcohol. A small shot of whiskey was enough to make the strongest of their number drunk. For one of them to drink half a bottle would be fatal, a thing that the early colonists soon discovered and used to great effect against the natives in the early stages of the war.

Gantry's eyes were attracted to a young girl standing beside the spring. She was beautiful even by earth standards. Her skin was almost white, with a deeper hue of red-yellow. Her body was sleek, with almost a golden quality in the Kingane sun. She shook her body, luxuriously, unself-consciously, casting off a fine spray of water from the tawny orange-black mane of hair that hung well past her shoulders. And looking at her, the source of his restlessness became clear to him.

As self-sufficient as he prided himself on being, he could not quell the feelings that come to a lonely man, to a man who looks in the mirror one morning, realizing somewhere deep inside, that he doesn't want to grow old alone.

In his heart, watching her move along the edge of the spring, he felt the meaning of the word freedom slipping away. He felt things stirring within him he had long since thought dead, buried. His pride had cut him off from family, from settling down, but now he felt a stealing tide of emotion slipping over his being and, in that instant, he knew he was lost.

He rose slowly and approached an old man who had not entered the water. He was the leader, an old man with one eye gone, a thick strip of lizard hide wrapped around his head covering the old wound.

"Do you speak English?" asked Gantry.

The old man, watching the young ones at their play, did not turn to look at him. He grunted once, affirmatively.

Gantry stared at the young girl. She was unmarried. The married Riyall woman wore a leather strip dyed blue around one ankle. Her ankles were bare. Gantry figured her to be somewhere around sixteen or seventeen. He kept his eyes on her, the words he knew he would speak damming up in his throat in a tumbled stream.

The old man turned to look at him, fixing the man with his expressionless Riyall stare.

And in that moment, as Gantry turned to look at him, turned and looked, he was almost able to stop himself. He remembered the times he had sworn to the buyers who came to buy his stefel harvest, sworn to them that he'd never touch a Riyall woman. Call it racial prejudice, or simply racial fear, he'd sworn he'd never degrade himself with a Riyall woman. He'd always told himself the colony company would get white women moved in some day, always told himself he could wait until then to relieve biological back pressure. He was about to make a liar out of himself.

Five years he'd waited, five years while the colony company had promised women were coming. They were a long time coming and there were a lot of men, men like Droble

who lived fifty miles from Gantry, Droble with two Riyall
women, who couldn't wait.

"I want her," said Gantry, the words finally coming out.

"She-daughter-oldest-of mine," said the old man, in broken English.

"How much?" asked Gantry, committed to it now.

Not knowing the word, the old one pointed at Gantry's
chest. "Bkaksi!" said the old man and he turned his head
and motioned at the girl. She came up to his side and he
said several words to her in his own language. She took the
news calmly, standing silently by the old man, gazing at
Gantry with that dead, expressionless Riyall look on her
face.

Gantry did not understand.

"How much?" repeated Gantry and he tried to indicate
by gestures that he wanted her.

The old man nodded and touched his own chest. He
fingered his snowfur lizard shirt and pointed at Gantry's
chest.

"That," said the old man and he made smoothing motions
along his shoulders and arms.

"The shirt?" asked Gantry, fingering the heavy work shirt.
He made a gesture as if taking it off and offering it to him.

The old man nodded and pushed her toward him. She
walked toward him and stood beside him, turning to face
her father.

Gantry pulled the shirt off over his head and handed it
over. The old man took it, folded it several times, laid it
upon the ground, arranging it carefully and then sat down
on it. He then turned away from them, the matter dismissed
from his mind.

Gantry stood there for a little while, the enormity of what
he had just done finally sinking in. He turned to look at the
young Riyall girl beside him. She did not seem upset or
nervous. It seemed to be of little importance to her, taking

the fact of her having to go with him as a matter over which she had neither control nor an opinion.

Gantry turned and began walking away, the Riyall girl moving along behind him, following five paces behind as was customary in her culture. The walk back to the cabin seemed to last an eternity to Gantry who seemed to be in a kind of shock, a kind of irrational fear. He had no idea what to expect from her. No idea then, but he soon found out.

She was more than he had ever expected. At first, he told himself it was sex that had prompted him to buy her, that he was not lonely, but even that lie fell away. He was lonely, and she filled that void. She wasn't human. He could never quite think of her that way, never get involved with her he told himself, but there were times when the difference seemed small, insignificant.

Although she seemed to show no emotions of her own, she was quick to perceive his. She seemed in some strange way related to the stefel dogs, having that kind of sensitivity, a turning outward with little directed at herself. She seemed to accept things passively—her personality suited to fit him and not her. She seemed to honor him and respect him in ways he himself could not quite understand. Her body seemed to exist to please him, her hands so soft and yielding in his, at times playful, coy almost when she sensed he needed some kind of resistance, when she sensed he needed something to oppose him.

But she had a will of her own in matters that did not directly affect him. He had discovered with a kind of shock that the trade, that the ceremony of giving a shirt for her was as binding as any marriage ceremony on any of the planets. And one day, why he never knew, after six months of their being together, after six months of sharing the same bed, he loaded her in the all-terrain vehicle and took her the 260 miles to the nearest hospital, and there, he had her placed in surgery so that she might have his children. What drove him to that, he could never quite say. It was not something he was sure he wanted for himself. In fact, the idea filled him with a kind of quiet terror. As if a child would be proof of his crime, a crime that was no crime on Kingane, but an act that still disturbed his spirit, that troubled his sleep as she lay beside him.

In a way, he supposed, in some sort of meaningfully twisted way, he was doing it for her, as if he was fulfilling some sort of obligation to her.

He remembered how she had touched him as the doctors wheeled her away to surgery and he had been reminded of a dog that one sends to a vet to have put to sleep. In that blank stare of hers, so guileless, so direct, he saw the pet dog, unsuspecting, trusting perfectly in your love even up until that moment when the needle breaks the skin and the long sleep begins.

In spite of his toughness he found tears in his eyes. The wrongness of his actions sat very heavily upon him, and deep inside, trapped within as deeply as he was trapped without, he knew he had as much power to stop it as he had to stop the clouds overhead.

The trip back to the cabin was a silent one, an uneasy trip, with Gantry sitting as far away from her as possible. He knew she was in pain, but he could not bring himself to touch her, to offer her any comfort. He was not so sure, now that she was fertile, now that he had made it possible for them to have children, if he did not hate her. He had long since stopped thinking of her as a possession. At times, it seemed as if he belonged to her.

Things went on as before, his life a flow of conflicting feelings, a flow of emotions he could no longer control. It seemed to him, like the stefel dogs that he fed, that he could never really own her. Her alienness was always between them. Her customs were strange, her manner unlike that of his race. And she was guided by this alien quality, this tradi-

tional way so unlike his own, to live in a way he could not
hope to touch or change. There were certain things between them. She would not eat at the table, eating instead on
the floor, after the manner of her people. Then, too, like a
raccoon on earth, she washed every morsel of food she ate.
There was something very animal, very alien about her as
she swished a slice of bread in a saucer of water before eating it. He had beat her for that once, but it made him uncomfortable to see her sitting across the table from him, not
eating, staring in the Riyallian way. In a way, it was how
she expressed her anger, if indeed she ever experienced it.
He sensed her displeasure and, once, when he had been par-
ticularly cruel, he thought he heard a trilling sound, a
throaty vocalization like the death rattle of the stefel dogs.
He thought perhaps it was her way of crying. But he could
never be sure.

And they had a child, a boy.

Often when the pebble storms of winter kept him inside,
he sat before the heating unit watching the boychild
crawling across the floor. She sat motionlessly on the other
side of the room, sitting there like some ill-conceived statue,
lost in streams of thought he could never touch, moving
with memories he never could share.

He talked her tongue so poorly, he could not make her
understand and she spoke no English, seemingly would not
allow herself to learn it. There were times, holding his
young son, staring into the child's eyes, blue and single-
pupiled like his own, when he wanted to talk to her, to tell
her the things and dreams within him. It was never to be.

The days passed silently for them while all around them,
like silt deposited by a flooding stream, the immigrants to
the planet continued to come. Women, children, entire fami-
lies moving to Kingane, now safely settled by those who
went before them. And as the years rolled by, towns were

born and with them came the civilization that had brought them. Gantry noticed it gradually, the weeks when the trail beyond the end of his land became full of travelers whereas, before, he rarely saw more than one or two people a month. One day he stood on the hill behind his cabin and he could see houses going up, maybe two or three miles away, and it was then that he knew a moment of unease, of dread. His own people had caught up with him.

A week later, finding himself dissatisfied, unaccountably restless, he took her into the new town that had sprung up almost overnight just ten miles from his cabin. In a way, his taking her there was a part of the blindness that had grown around him. He'd been with her so long, got so familiar and comfortable around her in their quietly spent years together, it had faded from his mind that she was an alien, that she might not be welcome.

He'd dressed her in a bright dress, purchased from the harvest buyers who stopped three times a year to buy his harvest of stefel tissue. But he had forgotten her customs, as unchangeable as the blue-green sky above. When they walked across the sidewalks, she followed him, moving behind him at her customary five paces. And in the eyes of those he met, in the eyes of those townspeople, he knew how she would look to them. He felt an anger rising in him. He heard comments from the people on the street, nothing direct, nothing he heard quite clearly, but he knew what they were saying about him, knew what they were thinking about her.

She saw the darkness in his eyes, when he turned to look at her, and without a word she turned and walked back to their landcar and got in to wait for him. She took it as she took all things, silently, matter-of-factly. But there was no way she could change who she was. He followed her and got into the landcar, driving away from the town, looking neither to the left nor right but aware that people had moved out of buildings to look at her, to look at them, and it burned into him with a bitterness and a loss that he knew would never stop. And he was never to take her into town again.

He knew then how it would be. When the stefel buyers decided they could no longer afford to visit each stefel rancher individually, when the buyers decided to open up an office in town where the ranchers could bring in their harvest, he knew his life, his aloneness, was lost to him.

At harvesttime, when he took his tank, now fitted with wheels, into town to sell his crop of tissue, he could sense the barrier between himself and the others of his kind. As he waited in the outer offices, waiting until his wagon was weighed and unloaded, the others sat apart from him as if he was a man of their race who was somehow not of their race. And the way women of his own kind passed their eyes over him, as if he were something unclean, filled him with a chill that seized him by the heart.

One day he met Droble at the weighing office, Droble who had two Riyall women. And as Gantry sat there, he listened to the talk around him. The men were talking about the changes around them, about the men who had pioneered this land. The pioneers were sending their Riyall women back into the wild lands from which they had come, sending away their half-breed children, sending them back to their own kind; at least, the ones with any brains were was what the men said. Droble turned pale as he heard their conversation, the idle chatter of men who had come to this world long after others had made it soft and easy for them. Droble stood up and stalked out of the office with a kind of hurtful violence. Droble still had his two Riyall women. Droble was the kind of man who needed people, a loner who still must be a part of society. Later, as Gantry was picking up his check for his crop, a man ran into the office shouting that Droble had just blown his head off in the mid-

dle of the street. The men in the office all dashed out to see
if for themselves. Gantry felt all the weight, the hope-
lessness of his mistakes come crashing down on him. It
might have been him out there on the street instead of
Droble.

He went home late that morning, very, very drunk. In the
morning, the last part of the night, the fatalness of his mistakes was apparent to him. He was no Charlie Droble and
he knew that the decision that Droble had made was an
easy one compared to the one he knew he would have to
make. Couldn't help but make.

But home in his own cabin, watching her and the boy eating, washing their food as was her custom, he found that he
did not have the strength to do it. He remembered back to
the time before his people had caught up with him. Had she
ever really held him tenderly? Was it his imagination that
had built her into a person, into a human being? Perhaps
she was a fabrication, a cold, emotionless creature he had
shaped with his imagination and his great need into more
than what she really was. She had never told him that she
loved him, for there was no way for her to communicate
that, to tell him that. But he had always assumed it, hadn't
he? Hadn't the care, the expressionless but gentle caring for
the boy convinced him of that?

The winter came and, with it, a deep gloom that settled
over the little cabin. There was no help for himself, Gantry
knew. He was committed to her, to his son, and he could not
sever those ties. She in her strange way sensed his great sorrow and, whether comprehending its source or not, seemed
to spend more time with the boy, less time with him, a thing
that Gantry experienced with a kind of relief. He had found
himself very critical of her lately, found himself very quick
to notice faults in her, faults that had never seemed obvious
to him before.

The meteor shower had lasted two days, longer than any

other shower he ever remembered. He sat at the table, eating his food, lost in the kind of misery that comes over a child forced to stay inside when it rains and there's nothing to do. He kept running it over and over in his mind, kept staring at them as they ate their meal, washing each bite of food first. The day before, the boy had said his first word. He had sensed it, had sensed that the boy was beginning to take on her personality even though the boy seemed to look a great deal like him. He had understood that first word of his and it was one of her language and not his.

It was funny how that bothered him the most. That the child would speak her words and not his. And it came to him, then, it came to him like a painful tearing sound, and he knew that he could not save himself. He knew he could not save her. There was no hope for her. No hope for him. There was nothing that could be done. Out the window he could see the shells of houses going up at the edge of his land, houses waiting till the summer and the right time to build them. His people had caught up with him.

He got up from the table slowly, his food untouched and he moved toward them. She knew what was to happen and in that unreadable face, he found the knowledge of what he was about to do. He lifted the boy away from the mat on the floor and cradling him against his chest, turned and walked back to the table. She sat motionlessly in the corner and, in that moment, he knew, he finally knew she was capable of emotion, that she had feelings of her own.

He pulled a chair up beside his and set the boy gently down upon the chair. He turned to her and, without a word, she knew that the boy's place would hereafter be at the table; she knew it by the sad unrelenting look on his face.

He took a piece of bread and put it unwashed into the boy's mouth. And then he heard it and turned to look at her. Her face was turned away, her shoulders motionless.

But he heard it and this time knew what it was. That melodious, birdlike sound, the way the creatures of Kingane cried, the sound the creatures of Kingane made when they were dying.

But he had his back hardened against it and would not relent, having made the judgment for the boy. But after the way of his own kind, his shoulders shook and he made the harsh, broken rasping sound, the way the creatures of Earth cried, the sound the creatures of Earth made when they were dying.

THE BLEEDING MAN

The medicine shaker, the bonebreaker. I have seen and been all these. It is nothing but trouble.

I have sat on the good side of the fire. I have cried over young women. It is nothing but trouble.

Miss Dow leaned against the observation window. Her stomach revolted and she backed away. Unable to quell the nausea rising within her she clamped a hand to her mouth.

Dr. Santell gently took her arm, led her away from the window and helped her to a couch facing away from the observation window.

Nausea passed; Miss Dow smiled weakly. "You did warn me," she said.

Dr. Santell did not return the smile. "It takes getting used to. I'm a doctor and immune to gore, but still I find it unsettling. He's a biological impossibility."

"Not even human," Miss Dow suggested.

"That's what the government sent you here to decide," said Dr. Santell. "Frankly, I'm glad he's no longer my responsibility."

"I want to look at him again."

Santell shrugged, lit a syntho. Together they walked back to the observation window. He seemed amused at her discomfort.

Again, Miss Dow peered through the window. This time it was easier.

A young man, tall and well-muscled, stood in the middle of the room. He was naked. His uncut black hair fell to the small of his back.

His chest was slit with a gaping wound that bled profusely; his legs and stomach were soaked with blood.

"Why is he smiling? What is he staring at?" she asked, unable to take her eyes off the figure before her.

"I don't know," said Dr. Santell. "Why don't you ask him?"

"Your sense of humor escapes me," said Miss Dow through tightly closed lips.

Dr. Santell grinned and shrugged. His synthetic cigarette reached the cut-off mark and winked out. The butt flashed briefly as he tossed it into the wall disposal.

"Doesn't everything?" suggested Dr. Santell, trying not to laugh at his little joke.

Miss Dow turned away from the window. Her look was sharp, withering. "Tell me about him," she snapped, each word like ice. "How did he get—that way?"

His amusement faded. He licked his lips nervously, nodded. "He has no name, at least no official name. We call him Joe. Sort of a nickname. We gave him that name about—"

"Fascinating," interrupted Miss Dow, "but I didn't come here to be entertained by some droll little tale about his nickname."

"Friendly, aren't you?" asked Santell, drily. A pity, he thought. If she knew how to smile, she might have seemed attractive.

"The government doesn't pay me to be friendly. It pays me to do a job." Her voice was cold, dispassionate. But she turned to face Dr. Santell in such a way that she would not see the bleeding man. "How long has he been like this?"

"It's all in my report. If you'd like to read it, I could—"

"I'd prefer a verbal outline first. I'll read your report later; I trust that it is a thorough one." She eyed him sharply.

"Yes, quite thorough," Dr. Santell replied, the polite edge in his voice wearing thin.

He turned away from Miss Dow, gazed in at the bleeding man. His words were clipped, impartial. "He is approximately twenty-three years old and has been as he is now since birth."

"Incredible!" said Miss Dow, fascinated in spite of herself. "All this is documented?"

"Completely. There is no possibility of fakery. Nor point either, for that matter."

"Just as you say," echoed Miss Dow. "What have you done to try to cure it? Is it some form of stigmata?"

Dr. Santell shook his head. "If this is stigmata, it is the most extreme case this world will ever see. Besides, it is inconceivable that a psychosomatic illness could cause such a drastic biological malfunction."

"But surely some sort of surgery?" began Miss Dow. "Some sort of chemical therapy would—"

Dr. Santell shook his head emphatically. "We've tried them all in the seven years he's been here. Psychochemistry, primal reconditioning, biofeedback—tried singly and together; none have had any effect. He's a biological impossibility."

"What is his rate of bleeding?" she asked.

"It varies," said Dr. Santell. "Somewhere between two and three pints an hour."

"But it's not possible!" exclaimed Miss Dow. "No one can—"

"He can and does," interrupted Dr. Santell. "He doesn't do anything normally. I can give you ten reasons why he should be dead. Don't ask me why he isn't."

Miss Dow turned her head around and stared at the silent figure standing in the center of the room. The bleeding man had not moved. The blood flowed evenly from the chest wound, gathering in a coagulating pool at his feet.

"I've had enough." She turned away from the window. "Show me to my office. I'm ready to read that report now."

Two hours later, the last page of Dr. Santell's report slipped from nerveless fingers. The bleeding man lay outside the parameters of human biology. By all rights he should have been dead, indeed, could never have lived. Her hands were a little unsteady as she punched in Dr. Santell's office on the videophone. His face appeared on the screen—and it was flushed.

"Report to me immediately," Miss Dow snapped.

"I doubt it, sweetheart," said Dr. Santell, grinning. "I'm off the case, remember?" He drank something out of a dark tumbler.

"You're drinking!" snapped Miss Dow.

"Now that you mention it," admitted Dr. Santell agreeably. He gave her a lopsided grin. "Perhaps you would care to join me?"

"You are a disgusting, undisciplined lout. And I should like to remind you that you are still responsible to me. You may be discharged from this case in your professional capacity, but your standing orders are to cooperate with me in any way possible."

"So I'm cooperating," muttered Dr. Santell. "I'll stay out of your way, you stay out of mine."

"I won't tolerate this!" she raged. "Do you realize to whom you are talking?"

Dr. Santell thought that over slowly. His face tightened. He did realize who she was. It sobered him a little. He took another drink from the tumbler to compensate.

"Are you sober enough to answer a few questions?"

He thought that over for a while too. "I'm drunk enough to answer any questions you have. I don't think I could answer them sober," he said.

"I am trying to be understanding," said Miss Dow, a note

of conciliation in her voice. "I realize it is quite natural for you to resent me. After all, I am responsible for your termination at this installation."

Dr. Santell shrugged it off. He took another drink from the tumbler.

"We're both professionals, Dr. Santell," reasoned Miss Dow. "We can't let emotional considerations enter into this. There is no place for emotion here. Our goals must be—"

"Hell! That's easy for you to say!" growled Dr. Santell. "You don't have any!"

"That's quite enough, thank you," said Miss Dow, pressing her lips together in a tight, angry line.

"No, it's not enough—" started Dr. Santell. "You can't—"

"The subject is closed!" she shouted.

There was an uneasy silence.

Miss Dow broke it by changing the subject. "What about his parents?" she asked.

"Didn't you read my report?"

"It said they committed suicide. It did not specify or go into any details. I have to know more than that. Your report was supposed to be thorough. You didn't list your sources of information on his early life, for one thing. I need to know—"

"Ask Nahtari. He can tell you everything," he said. He shrugged as if to say it was out of his hands.

"Who?"

"Nahtari. His uncle. He comes every week to visit his nephew. Nahtari used to exhibit him at the carnival until we discovered him and brought him here. If you'll turn to the financial report near the back, you will see that we pay him a small gratuity for the privilege of studying his nephew. We pay him by the week and he stops in to pick up his check and talk to his relative."

"Did you say talk to his relative?"

"Yeah. It's pretty strange. Nahtari talks to Joe every week

for an hour. I don't know if Joe understands anything that is said to him or even if Nahtari cares if he understands. I've never heard Joe respond in any way, not in the seven years I've been here."

"When does this Nahtari make his weekly visit?"

"He's here now, in my office. He brings me a pint of whiskey every week. Makes it himself. You'd never believe how good—"

Miss Dow hit the dial-out button viciously, cutting him off in midsentence.

She pushed the door open to Dr. Santell's office. She hadn't bothered to knock. Dr. Santell had his feet propped up on the edge of his desk. He held a drink in one hand and a deck of cards in the other. Across the desk from him sat a gray-headed old Indian dressed in faded blue jeans, cracked leather boots, and a tattered flannel shirt.

"I'll see your dime and raise you a dime," said Dr. Santell, slamming a dime onto the pile of change on the desk between them.

"Are you Nahtari?" demanded Miss Dow, coming into the room. The two studiously ignored her.

"It depends," said the old Indian, not looking up from his cards. "I'll meet your dime and raise you a quarter."

Dr. Santell bit his lip. "You're bluffing! I know you don't have that other ace!"

Miss Dow marched up to the desk and snatched the cards out of Dr. Santell's hands.

Dr. Santell pounded his desk in anger. "Stupid bitch! I had him beat!" He tried to collect the torn cards in his lap.

"Is she some kind of nut?" asked Nahtari, holding his cards out of harm's way.

Dr. Santell dumped the torn pieces of cards on the top of the desk and sighed. "Yeah. A government nut. She's in charge of Joe now."

Nahtari scowled and laid his cards face up on the desk. "And that means she wants to ask me about my relative."

"It certainly does," said Miss Dow. "Would you like to come to my office?"

Nahtari shrugged. There seemed no way to avoid it.

"You are owing me twelve dollars," he said to Dr. Santell as he rose to leave the room.

"Don't I always," growled Dr. Santell, staring at the ace that Nahtari had had after all.

"Sit down, Nahtari. This may take a while. I have a great many questions I want to ask you." She put a new cartridge in her tape machine and turned it on.

"If Dr. Santell had taken down all facts from before when I tell him, I would not having to be saying again," said Nahtari. "I get tired of telling the story and having no one taking down so I don't have to do all over again."

Miss Dow patted the tape machine. "Don't worry about it," she assured him. "This recorder will make a permanent record of everything you say. I guarantee you won't have to tell it again."

"You going to listen and take down no matter what?"

"Every word," she replied.

She started to ask a question but Nahtari held up his hand. "Let me tell whole story," said Nahtari. "It will be a saving of time and you can ask questions after if you have any. I want to get this over before too long. Got to catch Dr. Santell before he leave with my twelve dollar."

Nahtari scratched his chest over his right shirt pocket.

"That sounds all right to me," agreed Miss Dow. "Could you start with his parents? I'd like to know—"

"He killed them."

"What?" Miss Dow was stunned.

"He killed them," repeated Nahtari matter-of-factly. "I

was there the day he was born. His father and mother died within an hour of his birthing. He killed them."

Miss Dow was confused. "But how did it happen? How could—"

"You was not going to ask questions until I finished," accused Nahtari, dragging the back of his hand insolently across his nose.

Miss Dow settled back into her seat with a tight-lipped smile. She motioned for him to continue.

"His parents were medicine people. They were people of great power. My brother was one of the strong ones. They had this child stronger than them."

Miss Dow made a face. "You don't expect me to believe in primitive supersti—"

"I am expecting of you to keep your stupid mouth shut so this telling can be done and over with. I want to tell this so you will no longer pester me when I come to see my relative. I know all of your kind of government people. You harass a person—"

"Tell the story!" rasped Miss Dow. "For Christ sakes, just tell the story!" She drummed her fingers impatiently on the desk.

"My brother and his woman were filled with the sickness of the world. I knew that my brother did not want to live. His wife knew this and was content to go with him. Then when they had decided the road, she became heavy with child. They had no expecting of this. They became uncertain and did not know the way. But they could not change their decision for the living of the child. They went into the mountains, looking for their road. It was in the fifth month of the child in her belly."

Miss Dow sighed impatiently and settled back in her chair. It looked to be a long story, unrestricted by the inclusion of anything factual. Already she regretted asking him for information.

"They were high in the mountains. They laid down for dying but something strange happened. The child began speaking to them. The child was angry. They ran to the high places, to throw themselves off before the power of the child got too strong for them. But the child stopped them at the edge of the cliff and turned them around. The child forced them back down the mountain. And for four months, they were prisoners of the child."

"Are you seriously telling me that—" began Miss Dow with disgust.

Nahtari snorted contemptuously and passed his hands in front of his eyes. His eyes seemed to be focused on some far horizon. His voice mocked hers. "I just had a vision. I saw you and Dr. Santell embraced upon the ground and then suddenly crushed by a falling outhouse."

"I'm not laughing," said Miss Dow. She wasn't laughing.

"Somebody is," said Nahtari with a straight face. "I knew you was going to not let me finish the story and take it all down so I don't have to tell it again. Nobody ever lets me finish my story," complained Nahtari.

"Christ! I don't blame them!" said Miss Dow. "I've never heard such an outrageous piece of trash." She turned the tape machine off. "You may have all the time in the world but I haven't got time to listen to this idiocy!" She stood up and marched around the desk. "When you leave, shut the door."

Nahtari came around the desk and sat down in her chair. He tilted the chair back and rested his bootheels on the desk. He turned the tape recorder microphone around so that it pointed at him. He pushed the recording button and began talking into the machine.

"You bet this time, record is made of all the facts," he said and went on with the story. "For four months, they were prisoners of the child. Five days before he was born, the child began to fear leaving the belly. The fear did not last

long, but it lasted long enough for his father to put poison in
their food without the child's knowing. They ate this poison,
the mother, the father, and the child.

"The child felt the poison and changed it into water in his
belly. He felt great sadness in his heart and an anger because they did not want him to live. They did not want him
born into a world they had grown sick of. It was not their
right to choose for him because his power was greater than
theirs. He did not change the poison flowing through them
to water. His hatred was at them, for they had let the world
beat them. They began the agony of poison dying but they
could not die.

"I sat with them through this time. I sat with my brother
and sister-by-law and they told me these things through
their agony. They screamed to die but the child was punishing them for letting the world beat them. I, Nahtari, did not
want to see the child born into this world. I feared his coming. There was nothing I could do. He came to birth.

"It was not a child like expected. He bled. His chest was
bleeding. I had expected hot roaring fires. I had expected a
child of frightful appearance. It was but a small baby that
bled and could not talk.

"The father pulled the baby up and beat him into breathing. He laid the baby on the bed and went outside the
house. After a little while, my sister-by-law got to her feet,
swaying on dizzy legs, and she staggered out after him. I
tried to stop the bleeding of the baby chest but I was too
scared about my brother and sister-by-law. I ran outside.
They laid side by side in the black dirt of the garden. They
were dead and five days decayed.

"I took the little one into my home but the bleeding
sickened my old woman and she died. So I took the bleeding one to the traveling show. The white people there did
not sicken and die at the sight of his bleeding.

"In lines all round the tent they would stand to pay good

money to see the bleeding one. They all wanted to see him bleeding and they were not sickened by it and they did not die. But the government people came and took the bleeding one from me and made me sign little pieces of paper and gave me money so they could do what they do. I turned him over to the government ones and that is all there is to the story and it is the truth.

"Now I come every week to talk to him. I know he is too powerful to have a name. I am waiting for him. I am telling all this so I will not have to tell it again and so that this warning is given to all who would have dealings with him. He is not ready to do what he will one day do. Do not walk in his shadow. Leave him alone, for he is not you. For twenty-three years he has been gathering power. That is all I have to say."

He switched off the tape machine, smiling to himself because there was no one to hear it. He closed the door carefully behind him and went looking for Dr. Santell and his twelve dollars.

Miss Dow pushed open the door cautiously. She was not sure if she had the stomach for what she was doing. But making up her mind, she stepped into the room. She kept telling herself that he was perfectly harmless.

The drain in the center of the floor was stopped up with clotted blood. He stood in a shallow pool of his own blood. His body was motionless, his breathing just barely perceptible by a slight rising and falling of his chest. The blood flowed steadily to the floor.

"Can you hear me?" she asked nervously. She shut the door behind her. She kept her eyes on his face. He stared at her but gave no sign that he had heard her. He seemed to be in no pain, despite the stream of blood flowing down his chest.

"I'm not going to hurt you." She approached him slowly

with a small glass lab beaker. Averting her eyes slightly she placed the glass container below the wound.

She felt a little foolish for having spoken to him. It was obvious to her now that he was little better than a cretin and that he could not understand a word she said.

She stood there awkwardly, the glass beaker filling with his blood. The naked man seemed unaware of her presence, yet still she felt an unreasonable fear. There was something frightening about the still figure. Something threatening, otherworldly, in the steady flow of blood down his chest. He did not seem vulnerable. Rather it was as if the world were too insignificant for him to notice it.

She backed away from him with a full glass of his blood. She felt better with each step she took. He stared at her, no expression on his face, his eyes unusually bright. She had felt very uncomfortable under his stare.

Miss Dow had turned and started out the door, watching him all the while. Suddenly he moved. She turned quickly. Fear rose in her like a tide. The bleeding man cupped a hand beneath the wound in his chest.

Slowly, he brought his hands to his lips and drank of his own blood. Miss Dow fainted.

Dr. Santell found her in the doorway. A tiny, red pool of fresh blood was beginning to blacken on the floor beside her head. The glass beaker she had brought into the room was gone.

"What happened?" asked Dr. Santell, bending over the couch, his voice oddly gentle despite its gruffness. "Here— take a sip of this," he said, offering her a small glass of whiskey. "It'll steady your nerves."

She was too weak to refuse. The whiskey burned her throat and made her cough. He made her take another sip. It almost made her gag but it seemed to help. A touch of color reappeared in her face.

"He—he—he drank his own blood!" she whispered, tottering on the edge of hysteria.

Dr. Santell leaned forward eagerly. His features sharpened, his manner became intent and forceful. "Are you sure?" he demanded.

"Yes, I'm sure," she said with a trace of her normal sharpness.

"Are you sure—absolutely sure—he drank his own blood?" he asked again, impatiently. The answer seemed unusually important to him.

"Of course, I'm sure, damn it! It was absolutely disgusting!" She wrinkled up her nose. "That revolting animal did it on purpose. Just because I collected a beaker of his—"

Dr. Santell suddenly became greatly agitated. "You collected a glass beaker of his blood?"

She nodded, bewildered by his strange behavior.

"God! It's happened again," he muttered. "It's happened again!" A look of dread passed over his face.

"What the devil are you talking about?" demanded Miss Dow.

"When I heard you scream, I started running. I was the first one to reach you. You were sprawled in the doorway. There was a big bloodstain beside your head on the floor. There was no glass on the floor of the room and it wasn't in the hallway."

"Don't be ridiculous! I had it with me. Isn't this an awfully big fuss to be making over a—"

Dr. Santell turned his back on her and dialed security.

"Hobeman? This is Santell. Have room 473 searched for a glass beaker. Delay his feeding time if you have to, but find that beaker!" He shut off the viewscreen.

He looked at Miss Dow. Her face was blank with bewilderment. Before she could ask a question he began, "Something strange has developed in the last few weeks. Our monitors have been picking up unusual activity levels. They aren't sophisticated enough to tell us exactly what's happening but his heartbeat and galvanic skin responses have been fluctuating wildly."

"But what does that have to do with the glass?" asked Miss Dow.

"I'm coming to that. A week ago, during one of his strange activity levels, the observation port on the wall of his room disappeared."

Miss Dow's face registered shock. "Disappeared? How is that possible?"

Dr. Santell was grim. "I have no idea whatsoever. We found traces of melted glass on the floor of the room. But what disturbs me the most is that we could detect no coronary activity at the time of the disappearance. For two hours his blood was circulating but his heart wasn't functioning."

"He's not human, is he?" said Miss Dow.

"I don't know," said Dr. Santell, staring off into space. "I just don't know."

He pushed the carts through the door. The bleeding man stared at him as he had stared for the seven years he had been there.

"Soup's on, Joe," said the man with the feeding carts.

Two men hidden from view by the door were examining two streaks of melted glass on the floor.

"Hey, hold up there," said one of the men. "He's not to be fed until we've finished our search."

"I won't get in the way. What's disappeared this time?"

"Nothing important," grumbled one of the men. "Just a glass jar from the lab."

"Shame on you, Joe," said the cartman, waving a finger at the motionless figure in the center of the room. "You oughten to be stealing stuff like that." He opened the top of his cart and took out a pair of gloves.

"It won't hurt if I feed him, will it? I don't have to hose him down until you guys have finished," he said, pulling the gloves over his hands.

"Go ahead. We aren't going to find anything anyway."

The cartman opened a panel on the side of the cart and brought out a bowl of raw meat. He sat it on the floor in front of the bleeding man. From the other cart he got a large bowl of uncooked vegetables and a large wooden ladle.

He detached a water hose from the wall and started backing toward the bleeding man, uncoiling the hose as he walked. When he got to the end of the hose, he turned around.

The bleeding man had overturned the feeding bowls with his feet. He was drinking his own blood from cupped hands.

"This is what you are looking for," said Dr. Santell, handing Miss Dow a clipboard. "His blood type is O lateral. We've run hundreds of tests on it and it seems to be perfectly normal blood, a little more resistant to some diseases than ordinary blood but otherwise normal. It's too bad the government won't let us use his blood. He's a universal donor and, at the rate he produces blood, I'll bet he could supply Intercity all by himself."

"But that's just the point. We *are* going to use his blood," said Miss Dow. "We are going to use his blood," said Miss Dow, "and a lot more besides. That's why I was sent here to take charge of this case."

"The government's changed its policy, then?" asked Dr. Santell. "Why?"

"We've given transfusions of his blood to prisoners and it seems to have no bad effects. Tell me, you've studied him for seven years, do you have any idea how something like him is possible?"

Dr. Santell lit a synthetic cigarette slowly. He gave her a curious look.

"Did you listen to Nahtari's explanation?"

"That lunacy," sniffed Miss Dow. "I think we should pay a little more attention to a chromosomal-mutation theory than some wild story from some unwashed primitive like Nahtari."

Dr. Santell shrugged. "It doesn't really matter what caused it. I couldn't even make an educated guess. His version is the only evidence we have."

"Confine yourself to specifics, please," said Miss Dow. "What biological evidence do we have?"

"There is biological evidence pointing to chromosomal differentiation. He has sixty-four paired chromosomes. I have been unable so far to determine their exact structure. He seems to have all the normal ones. Technically, that makes him a member of our species, I suppose. But it's those extra chromosome pairs that are so unusual. They seem to be entirely new structures unlike anything we are familiar with. It must be something outside our experience. I think I pointed this out in more detail in my report."

"But technically, he is human?" asked Miss Dow.

"I would say he is," said Dr. Santell.

"Very well. Then I am going to give the final go-ahead on this project," said Miss Dow.

"And what project is that?"

"We're going to transfer him to the military dome at Intercity, where he will be dissected for tissue regeneration. Hopefully, his cellular matrix will produce like-functioning biological constructs."

"What!" Dr. Santell jumped to his feet. "You're not serious! That would be murder! Matrix reconstruction from tissue cultures has never advanced beyond the experimental stage! We don't have the technology yet to stimulate the reproduction of brain and nerve tissue! Good lord, woman, you can't seriously—"

"I am quite aware of our shortcomings in the field of tissue regeneration," said Miss Dow coldly. "For years, our work in this area has been little better than a waste of time and materials. We have yet to produce a successful unit with a well-developed nervous system. Nor have we been able to successfully clone an individual. These matters, however, are not relevant to this particular case."

"Not relevant! You'll kill him! And to what purpose? A line of research that you yourself admitted has been a waste of time!" stormed Dr. Santell, his face flushed with anger.

"Be careful, Dr. Santell," she cautioned him. "I don't think I am happy with your choice of words. We are not going to kill him. Many of our first tissue-regeneration experiments are still alive—alive after a fashion, that is. Their bodies still function, their cells still grow, it is only their minds that are dead." She smiled.

"It's still murder! You have no right!" Dr. Santell looked away from Miss Dow. He had suddenly realized that the things he was saying could be considered treason.

"When's the last time you had an attitude check, Dr. Santell?" asked Miss Dow. "I almost thought I heard you say something that was opposed to the wishes of our government. You did agree that my patient can be made ready for transport by tomorrow morning, didn't you?"

"Of course," said Dr. Santell. "He will be ready."

"And did I hear you use the word *murder*, Dr. Santell? I *did* hear you use the word! I'm sure General Talbot will be most interested in your attitude."

Dr. Santell turned and began walking out of the room. He knew that he was in trouble and nothing he could say would make it any better.

"Dr. Santell!"

He turned to look at her.

"I'm not really all that hard to get along with," said Miss Dow. "You have a reputation of being a brilliant scientist. I've handled your type before. I am willing to overlook a small measure of eccentricity. But I draw the line at treason."

His expression remained blank.

"It's only natural that you're defensive about your patient after seven years," she soothed. "You have personalized him, lost your objectivity. But you must know as well as I do that the bleeding man is a brainless vegetable, hopelessly retarded since birth. You can see that, surely?"

Dr. Santell stared at her wordlessly.

"It would be a lot easier for me," she continued, "if I had your cooperation on this thing. You've had seven years' experience on this project and you could help us smooth over any rough spots we might encounter. This isn't exactly a normal case. It will undoubtedly require special procedures —procedures that your cooperation will make possible." She smiled at him. "My report could be a very positive one. It depends on you."

Dr. Santell forced himself to smile. "Believe me," he said, "I shall cooperate in any way I can. I apologize for my behavior."

Miss Dow nodded. "Good. Now, how much blood could, let's say, ten of his regenerations produce in a forty-eight-hour period?"

Dr. Santell began punching up figures on his desk calculator.

The bleeding man continued to drink. The men studying the glass streaks on the floor had fled.

A security guard unlocked the door and looked into the room. The bleeding man did not seem aware of the other's presence. A call went out for Dr. Santell.

Dr. Santell, followed by Miss Dow, arrived just in time to see the heavy door buckling outward.

"He's gone berserk!" screamed Miss Dow, as the door was battered off its hinges. The bleeding man walked through the wreckage of the door. He advanced upon them, a crimson trail of blood behind him on the floor.

Miss Dow fled, screaming. Dr. Santell stood his ground. The bleeding man brushed him lightly as he walked past. He looked neither to the left nor right. He strode down the corridor, moving quickly, relentlessly.

Dr. Santell ran in front of him and tried to push him to a halt. His hands slipped, coming away blood soaked. His efforts to stop him were futile. Through the plastiglass corridor walls he could see the security guards gathering around Miss Dow at the corridor exit. Dr. Santell took hold of the bleeding man's arm and tried to drag him to a stop but found himself being dragged instead. The bleeding man did not even break stride.

Miss Dow stood within a cordon of security men. Dr. Santell knew what she would order them to do even before the bleeding man smashed through the exit door.

"Aim for his head!" she shouted.

A burst of stunner fire took the bleeding man full in the face. He walked several steps, then toppled.

Dr. Santell rushed to his side and put a hand on his chest. "He's still alive," he muttered to himself.

"Good shooting, men," congratulated Miss Dow. "A couple of you men carry the body down to the lab.

"Is there very much damage to his head?" she asked. "Is he still alive? Not that it matters. We can't risk another episode like this. We might as well do the dissection here. It'll make him easier to handle. We'd have to ship him frozen anyway, now that we know more about his capabilities."

The security men carried the body away.

"He's still alive," Dr. Santell said, pronouncing each word slowly and distinctly. "He's very much alive."

Miss Dow had a surgical gown on and a mask. "Are you sure you can handle the dissection all by yourself, Dr. Santell? I could fly someone in to assist."

"Quite sure," said Dr. Santell, bending over the still form on the surgery table. "I'll begin soon. You'd better leave now."

"I'll be waiting at the military base in Intercity for the body," said Miss Dow. She came over to the table and stood beside him. Her voice was cold and emotionless as usual. "You realize I still must report your treasonable remarks to General Talbot."

Dr. Santell nodded, not looking in her direction.

"However, your behavior has shown marked improvement. That too will be noted in my report. Trying to stop this creature single-handedly in the corridor like you did was a very brave, if somewhat foolish, thing to do. You realize after that the matter is out of my hands. General Talbot will be the one deciding, not I. Perhaps, after a short period of retraining, you may even be reassigned. A man of your reputation, I'm sure, will find it very easy to rejoin the fold. Only a fool—or a traitor—bucks the system."

Dr. Santell seemed not to be listening. He stuck a needle into the arm of the body on the dissection table.

"What a shame a body like that should have no mind," mused Miss Dow. "Just think of the power he must have in order to smash through those doors like he did."

"Yes," Dr. Santell replied tonelessly.

Miss Dow pulled her mask off and turned to leave.

"Wait," said Dr. Santell. "Before you go, could you hand me that box of clamps under the table here?"

She bent over and looked under the table. "I don't see any—"

His scalpel sliced through her right carotid artery. Her body jerked convulsively and she crashed heavily to the floor.

"Yes," said Dr. Santell with a strange look on his face. "It is always a shame to find a good body with a defective mind."

It took him a little over two hours to dissect her. By the time he finished, the stimulant he had injected into him had brought the bleeding man back to consciousness.

As he was putting her dismembered body into the liquid-nitrogen packs for shipping, he kept his eyes on the body of the bleeding man. The body sat up slowly and opened its eyes. The head swiveled and the eyes regarded him. The eyes were alive with raw intelligence. The body slid off the table gracefully and stood up, the wound on his chest completely healed.

"I knew," said Dr. Santell. "I knew."

The medicine shaker, the bonebreaker. I have seen and been all these. It is nothing but trouble.

I have sat on the good side of the fire. I have cried over young women. It is nothing but trouble.

These are the words I heard written in his skin. He made me kill her. I had to do it. I am not sorry. I knew. That is enough, knowing.

—Paul Santell

((This suicide note was found near the charred body of Dr. Paul Santell, who, Intercity Police say, apparently soaked himself with an inflammable liquid and then set himself afire. Dr. Paul Santell, twice recipient of the Nobel Prize in psychochemistry, police report, had been experiencing . . . —excerpt from Intercity Demographic Area Telepaper.))

K38 The bleeding man cured of bleeding, walked without

haste toward the door leading outside. He remembered the taste of blood, he who no longer had need of it. He pushed the door open and stepped outside. The sky pulled at him but he resisted for that last little moment. His feet touched the ground. His lungs filled with air. His eyes danced on the horizons of the world. Raising his hands into the air, he let the sky pull him away from the earth. He took the air in his lungs and thrust it out with a shout. Silently his lips formed words.

And then he had no more need of air and words. His fingers curled into the hands of the sky. He disappeared in a cloud.

He Who No Longer Bleeds is gone. He will return. To bleed again.